**This book is to be returned on or before
the last date stamped below.**

24·1·08
THURSDAY

30/9/14

D0726606

LIBREX

Oth...

THE BA...
THE CRY OF...
JUNK
KITE
TIGER, TIGER

In Puffin

AN ANGEL FOR MAY
THE EARTH GIANT

MELVIN BURGESS

LOVING APRIL

PUFFIN BOOKS

PUFFIN BOOKS

Published by the Penguin Group
Penguin Books Ltd, 27 Wrights Lane, London W8 5TZ, England
Penguin Putnam Inc., 375 Hudson Street, New York, New York 10014, USA
Penguin Books Australia Ltd, Ringwood, Victoria, Australia
Penguin Books Canada Ltd, 10 Alcorn Avenue, Toronto, Ontario, Canada M4V 3B2
Penguin Books (NZ) Ltd, Private Bag, 102902, NSMC, Auckland, New Zealand

Penguin Books Ltd, Registered Offices: Harmondsworth, Middlesex, England

First published by Andersen Press Ltd 1995
Published in Puffin Books 1996
8

Copyright © Melvin Burgess, 1995
All rights reserved

The moral right of the author has been asserted

Made and printed in England by Clays Ltd, St Ives plc

British Library Cataloguing in Publication Data
A CIP catalogue record for this book is available from the British Library

ISBN 0–140–36983–X

With special thanks to Gilly Wilkinson

This book is for Avis

1

The swans stood on the dark mud. There was a low mist over the water and none of them took much notice of a small grey boat that floated towards them from the jetty on the other side until it was almost upon them. The flow of water was quite strong. One or two of the swans watched anxiously as the boat cut a jerky line against the current towards them.

The swans often came to roost here on the river when the tide was out. Sometimes there were just a few, sometimes as many as thirty or forty. Tonight there were nearly a hundred. April was sure she'd be able to catch one this time.

April lay inside the boat, covered by an old blanket camouflaged with twigs and leaves. Several days ago she had tied one end of a piece of rope to an old boat that lay stranded in the mud on the other side. Then she had swum back with the other end, which she passed through a hole drilled in the prow of her own little rowing boat. Now she lay out of sight, pulling the rope through the hole and gliding unseen towards the roosting birds.

April was so pleased and so certain of her plan that she began to chuckle to herself as she got close. It was hard work pulling in that position with her elbows bruising on the hard boards. The rope cut into her hands but she barely noticed. She could see the swans through the hole in the prow. The stupid birds hadn't a clue! Soon she would ground herself on the mud and then leap out with her blanket.

The boat silently embedded itself in the mud. April seized her blanket and leapt to her feet with a cry of

1

delight. The swans right by her jumped in the air; one fell over in fright. She laughed for joy and lurched forward. But the boat was unsteady. It sluiced under her feet; she jerked sideways. The bow pulled itself out of the mud and the little craft spun round, pulling the rope out of the hole with a rapid purr. April flung out her arms, yelped, pitched backwards and fell with a great splat on her back in the mud. She sat up, spitting mud, to see the backs of a hundred swans running, their wings tipping the mud, their black feet padding frantically as they stretched their long necks into take-off. The air was filled with their splashing feet, the loud fluting whistle of their pinions and above all with the thudding of those great wings in the air. Suddenly the boat began to drift away. April flung an arm at it but it slid past, the rope running freely out of the bow. She fell back down and screamed in anger at the fleeing swans. The air was a-roar with feathers and wings but the girl heard nothing but a dull echo of her own cries.

April was deaf.

She had to swim back across the river and then crawl through the mud on the other side. The mud was deep, black and smelly. A woman walking her dog caught her just as she was emerging and screamed. The dog barked; April barked back and the dog jumped in surprise, and barked delightedly.

'Oh, April,' complained the woman, recognising the bark. April took no notice of her. She wiped her eyes free of mud and began to walk along the bank to find her boat.

It was growing dark by the time she got home. She lived in a brick house overlooking the railway station. It used to be the Station Master's house, but the Station

Master – her father – had died eight years ago. Now just she and her mother lived there, together with April's many pets. Her favourite pet was Silas, a big cob swan who adored April and would have followed her everywhere if she'd let him. It was April's greatest desire to catch a mate for Silas and have a family of swans to walk after her up and down the village streets, but so far her plans had come to nothing. Silas lived roped by the foot to a dog kennel outside the house and he came up to her hissing with his mouth open and bowing his head. April patted him and thought . . . another time.

Inside she found her mother arranging her hat in the mirror in the hall. The mud had dried to a powdery skin by this time. April, flaking mud on the grubby linoleum and trying not to laugh, tried to creep up and take her by surprise but as always her mother heard her coming. There were so many sounds April had no idea existed – the creak of her feet on the boards, the squeak of the door as she opened it, even the bang as the door swung to behind her and the thud of her own feet. But she heard her mother's scream all right when she caught sight of her in the mirror.

'Ahhhh! . . . Oh my God!' screamed her mother. April, who thought she really had crept up without her hearing, smiled delightedly. 'What are you trying to do, kill me?' Mrs Dean leaned back with her hand on her heart and glared at her. 'Have you been out like that? Have you been walking the streets like that? Bloody hell, bloody hell . . .!'

She dashed across and dragged her daughter outside and made her stand in the grass. 'What are you trying to do? We have a reputation to keep up . . . walking about like that . . . covered in filth . . .' Her mother raged as she disappeared into the kitchen for a pail of cold water. Silas settled down outside his kennel to watch.

'. . . people seeing you wandering about covered in filth . . . what if the railway authorities get to hear about it? We'll be chucked out, that's what, we're only here on sufferance . . .' April's mother jerked back the bucket and sent cold water flying all over the girl, who cried out in shock.

'Serve you right,' said her mother primly. She dashed back in for a second bucket. April cringed back, but the older woman just set it in front of her with a wash rag. 'Now clean up!'

The mud began to smell again as it got wet and Mrs Dean wrinkled her nose in disgust. April soaked the cloth and squeezed it on her skin. She washed in a leisurely manner, watching the muddy water wash down her and drip off her clothes. She glanced at her mother once or twice, then ignored her. Mrs Dean rattled on, getting angrier and angrier as April got wetter, but all the girl could hear was a blurred buzz, a distant voice in a locked room she could never enter.

April could lip read well enough but when her mother was angry she spoke so fast that April just turned off. Soon she forgot her mother altogether and began to daydream about the swans gathering on the misty water.

Mrs Dean, who was in a hurry, stamped her foot in exasperation as April ground to a halt and gazed over the road, seeing nothing. She could swear the girl did it on purpose, but April looked so calm and self-absorbed that she stopped shouting for a moment and stared. Her daughter could be so good looking when she wasn't moving about like a restless dog or staring at you like a mad thing. She was a lovely, dumb animal that knew nothing. At moments like this Mrs Dean could have wept for pity. In any other girl such good looks would be an asset but for April there was no future. The girl couldn't talk. She couldn't even read or write.

Mrs Dean noticed suddenly how April's wet clothes clung to her skin. She waved her arms to attract attention. 'You've left your bra off again,' she accused. April looked down at her breasts in alarm, covered them with her arms and turned away from the road. 'Going around like that . . . people'll see,' her mother scolded. 'Do you want them to see you like that?' she snapped angrily nodding at the wet blouse which left so little to the imagination.

Mrs Dean looked anxiously up and down the road for Peeping Toms. Some way off, in the cooling spring air, came the soft chuff, chuff, chuff of the steam train heading up the line towards them. With a tut, Mrs Dean dragged her daughter inside and found a bath towel to wrap around her shoulders.

'You stay hidden in here. Wandering around like that. Wait till all the passengers have gone before you come out and clean up. Even better, go and do it in the coal shed. Mind you put a plank or something down to stand on!' She dashed back indoors, shoving her girl before her. 'And then straight to bed, young lady, you hear me?' she snapped. She re-arranged her hat in the mirror and ran out again in time to catch the train to Redcliffe to begin her weekend job.

Inside, April ignored her mother's instructions to stay in the kitchen and walked up to her room, dripping black water behind her as she went up the bare wooden steps. She held the towel around her neck and watched the train pull into the station below her, belching steam and smoke. Doors opened and slammed shut with a soft 'puff'. The smell of coal and hot metal drifted up to her.

5

April loved the train. Soon the huge iron weight would pull away and the floor and walls would tremble.

She saw her mother standing on the platform and when they caught each other's eye, Mrs Dean waved frantically at her to get out of sight. April hurriedly ducked back into the room. She peeped out a moment later and her mother looked away and pretended it was nothing to do with her.

The doors all slammed, the train pulled away. April laid her cheek on the window pane to feel it rattle. She scanned the platform to see who was coming, and to her surprise saw two strangers. One was a pretty, well-to-do lady. The other was a boy a little younger than April, dressed in stiff grey clothes. Some sort of uniform. A porter was loading a pile of boxes, trunks and suitcases onto a trolley and then the little procession made its way out of the station and into the village. They had to walk right past April's window. As she watched them moving away from her, April forgot herself and began to shout at them, 'Where are you going? Where are you going? Are you coming to stay?' in a loud voice.

Tony's mother had insisted that he wear his school uniform for their arrival in the village. He tried to wear it proudly but he was ashamed really because he shouldn't be in it at all, now. After this, after everyone had seen that he was a St. Robin's boy, he could never wear it again.

As he walked along Tony kept his head down. Despite his school uniform, despite his mother's insistence that they make a proud entry into the village, he was sure everyone would know that they were poor people now. They would know for certain when they saw his mother and him enter their new home, which Tony was convinced would be a miserable hovel. They'd be lucky to get glass in the windows.

Home used to be a large, cool, brown house near a cemetery and farmlands. His father, who was rather large, waddled about comfortably and took no nonsense, either from his servants or his only son. His wife appeared to follow his every whim but really she did as she liked as soon as he left the house for work at the bank.

Tony was only there for the holidays. The rest of the time he was a boarder at St. Robin's. The school was hard. If you stepped out of line you were beaten – by the masters, by the prefects, by the other boys. He had to fag for one of the prefects, Willis, who made him shine his shoes, cook his toast, even sit on the lavatory seat to warm it up in the morning. When he did get home in the holidays he got so bored in the end that he actually looked forward to school. But as soon as he walked through the gates and his heart sank like a dead thing, he knew that it was just a mirage and he would a thousand times rather be anywhere else than here.

That was the old life. This was the new life – the village that crouched prettily behind the railway station and the smelly mud of the river. Tony's father had left them, they had no money and everything was going to be different. Tony would have given anything to get his old life back.

Clouds of midges bobbed around Tony's head and the prickly hair at the back of his neck itched, but he wouldn't scratch. He risked a look around about him; there was no one to be seen so he raised his head and quickly scanned the little houses ahead, trying to guess which would be theirs. It was at this moment that a horrible noise came from behind them. Tony froze in horror and glanced back. Someone mad was screaming at them from the upstairs window of a house next to the station. It was a girl. She was covered in mud, her hair was dried into rat's tails and she was hooting and yelling at them. Horrified, Tony stared up at her.

His mother paused a second in her step and then smoothly continued on her way, waving a hand elegantly at the midges in her face. The porter, wheeling the loaded trolley behind them, put down his load and looked back.

'Oh, that's April. Don't mind her.' He tapped his ear. 'Deaf and dumb, see.' He turned and yelled up to her, 'Don't holler, April. Shshshsh . . .' He mimed. The girl stopped shouting. 'Little devil finds out everything, don't ask me how,' he added to Tony's mother.

'Poor child,' murmured Barbara Piggot, without looking back. Out of the corner of his eye Tony glared hatefully at the muddy face in the window. She was like a broken trumpet announcing the arrival of two donkeys.

The new house was a damp cottage on the edge of town, overhung by trees. One side of it looked as if it had fallen down. The porter was confused; he couldn't work out what people like this were doing there.

'Is this the right one, are you sure?' Assured that it was, he stood awkwardly waiting. Mrs Piggot sighed, took out her purse and gave him a shilling.

'Thank you, ma'am. If you need anything . . .' He touched his cap and walked away.

'I thought we couldn't afford to do that sort of thing,' Tony said.

Mrs Piggot pursed her lips. 'He was expecting it, darling.'

8

'Are we going to have to buy poor people's clothes now?' he asked her.

'Oh, dear, I do hope not. Now be a dear and bring a couple of suitcases in and we'll have a look round, shall we?'

The house was horrible. There was no dining room; they'd have to eat in the tiny, stone-flagged kitchen like servants. There was a huge ugly white sink and a scrubbed table and three chairs, one of which was broken. There was dust and dirt and grease. There was a cupboard on the wall with mould growing inside it.

'We'll need to buy plates and things,' observed Mrs Piggot.

There was a small sitting room at the front and up a narrow stairway, two tiny bedrooms.

'There're no carpets,' said Tony. His mother arched her thin brown eyebrows. They went to unpack the bedding from the trunk. Later, on his way to bed, Tony asked, 'Are we going to have to live here for long, Mother?'

She was sitting on a tiny sofa in the sitting room, arranging her make-up on the seat beside her. 'We'll just have to see how we get on,' she smiled at him over her shoulder.

'Are you going to get a job? Will you earn a lot of money? I mean . . . can you do anything?' Tony wanted to know.

Barbara Piggot laughed softly. 'I have all sorts of talents you don't even dream about, darling. Don't worry, we won't be here for ever. It may take some time, that's all. In the meantime, we'll just have to make the best of it.'

'Will I have to start in the village school?'

She bit her lip. 'No. You'll be way beyond all of them.

I hope, anyway. We'll find something else for you to do. Now do run along, dear. I have so much to think about.'

Tony tramped upstairs and lay down in the little bed at the back of the house and looked out of the window that had no curtains. Down below him, his mother waited until she heard the springs of the bed squeak as he climbed in. Then she put her hand to her mouth and began to cry silently.

2

Tony lay in bed as long as he could the next day. When he got downstairs his mother was out. There was a note on the table for him: 'Gone Shopping'.

'Good.' Tony was starving. They'd had hardly anything to eat the day before. He passed the time by going round the house searching in the cupboards and drawers and in the outside toilet and coalhouse.

His mother came back shortly with her arms full of packages and her face bright. 'Sugar,' she cried, flinging a triangular blue packet on the table. 'Tea, bacon, cheese, bread and butter, milk. Everything you need for a civilised breakfast – well, semi-civilised, anyway. Plates will have to wait.' She was bright and breezy. Tony watched her as she unwrapped her packets and began pulling hunks off the bread and spreading the butter onto it with an old knife he'd found in a drawer.

'How much money do we have?' he asked.

She smiled nervously. 'All this is on credit, darling. There's more coming. Mr Riley the grocer was very obliging. He's bringing the rest along in his van at twelve after he closes up. I don't suppose,' she added thoughtfully, 'that he'll be quite so keen when he realises we're actually living here. But of course it'll be too late by then.' She smiled at Tony, who looked away.

Tony and his mother ate their breakfast out of the wrappers as if it was a picnic. He felt better with the food inside him. He kept looking out of the window, remembering the river he'd seen as they got off the train the night before. He wanted to explore, get out in the early

11

summer sunshine. But he was ashamed to be seen creeping out of that squalid little house.

'I'm dying for a cup of tea,' sighed his mother, eyeing the heavy black stove. 'Mr Riley said he'd bring us a bag or two of coal, just to get us through the weekend. So obliging.'

Tony didn't mention that there was some coal in the coalhouse. 'How are you going to pay him?' he wanted to know.

'Well, your father can hardly cut us off without anything, I suppose. I have some news.' She smiled palely at him and rummaged in her bag. 'We had a telegram this morning. Uncle Bob is coming over tomorrow – to assess the situation, he says.'

Tony's heart jumped. 'He's got loads of money. You could have got as much food as you wanted,' he said eagerly.

'I don't know about that. It was Uncle Bob who helped your father arrange for this splendour surrounding us, to which we have to become accustomed.' Mrs Piggot waved her hand at the house around them. 'I'm not counting terribly on Uncle Bob, darling.'

Nevertheless, she was determined to make another shopping expedition before the shops all closed. It was Saturday, and they only stayed open till lunchtime.

'We have to decide what to eat for two whole days,' she said anxiously. She stroked her neck and murmured, 'And cook it, too . . .' in a worried voice.

'Can you cook?' enquired Tony.

'Well, I have supervised.'

'Oh . . . well, I've got something for you, then.' Tony got up to one of the cupboards where he had found just what they needed . . . a cookery book. 'Here you are,' he said handing it to her. ' "One hundred recipes for a shilling". Should be useful.'

'Just the thing,' replied his mother evenly, not sure whether he was teasing her. 'So many new adventures, Tony. And, of course, you'll have to help too.'

'Not cooking, surely?'

'I've no intention of becoming your skivvy, darling. Now then, let's see ... Who'd have thought it possible to make a meal at such little cost? For a family of four, too, it says here. Hope springs eternal.' Mrs Piggot flicked through the pages. She used to have a cook. She sometimes descended to tell the cook what to cook, but never how to do it. She was not in her element.

'Oh, look – fish soup. I love fish soup! Mrs Parnell used to make a delicious soup with parsley and croutons and that sort of thing. It says here,' she added, frowning at the print, 'that you can make a very tasty, cheap and nourishing soup with a fish's head! Who'd have thought it? Would you have thought that, Tony?' She read a few more lines before closing the book with an excited slap.

'Do you know, they have some sort of fish place here in Cibblesham? I smelt it ... saw it ... they pack it up or something. I'm sure it would be terribly fresh and cheap. Tony ... now, darling, I do want you to help me out. I'll be cook, you be the maid. Run along and see if they have any fish heads ... I expect we can even get them for nothing, it says here people often give them away. You can't miss it, it's just round from the church Follow your nose.'

But Tony would rather have died than be seen running down the street to beg fish heads for dinner. He wasn't sure he wouldn't rather die than eat them, either.

His mother frowned and stood up. She popped a last

scrap of bread into her mouth. 'Then I shall have to go myself.'

'Mother, you can't . . . it would be begging!'

'We can't be choosers, not now,' she told him pertly. 'You light the fire . . . we shall want to cook it I expect. Collect some wood from behind the house, I saw lots of it lying on the ground. We can make a cup of tea when I come back.' And to Tony's everlasting shame she got up and walked straight down the road to the fish packagers. He watched her as far as the corner, blushing red as if it were him out there. Then he dashed about to light the fire, breaking twigs from behind the house and tearing an old newspaper lining a drawer to get it going. With the bit of coal still in the coalhouse he had quite a satisfactory blaze going by the time his mother returned. She banged a huge newspaper parcel on the table. 'I got two!' she exclaimed triumphantly. 'Two huge ones, for free. We can eat for weeks!'

The fish heads were enormous and hideously ugly. Tony was certain he would never be able to eat them. They had great cold clammy eyes and wide mouths and wattles on their lips. His mother dived under the sink and emerged with a preserving pan. They got one of the heads in with much shoving and pushing and covered it with water. By this time the fire was going strongly and the dust on the hotplate was beginning to singe. Barbara was delighted.

'How clever! What an enterprising pair we are. I'm sure we'll manage.' They put the preserving pan on the hot plate and watched it cautiously. After fifteen minutes or so an ugly grey scum appeared and the head rose up in the water and peered at them, its eyes turning slowly white.

'There!' exclaimed Tony's mother with satisfaction.

'Delicious fish soup. It says in the book we have to wait till the flesh falls off.'

'Ugh!' Tony made a disgusted noise, but he was amused and giggled. It was like Scouts or something. 'I expect it'll take some time,' he said, looking at the monster in the pan.

'I expect so. Well, we can wait.' She smiled and took his hand. They stood together watching the fish bobbing up and down as the water began to boil.

The house by the station was so close to the river that early in the morning sheets of mist crept off the water and in through the doors and windows if you left them open. Once, she'd been able to open everything wide but these days, April only dared leave the top windows open when her mother was away. Her mother was always working – as a waitress during the day, in a pub at night and in a club over the weekend, when she stayed in Redcliffe with her sister. April always did as she was told when her mother was there in front of her, and always did exactly as she liked when her back was turned.

The damp got into the beds and sent growths of black mould up the walls. This morning the mist rose high enough to get in her bedroom window on the first floor. April was delighted; she loved the feel of the white air in the morning, as if she was still outdoors. She was up at dawn. First thing she went to the hen house to let the birds out and take the eggs. There were six this morning. April ate two and beat two more up in a bowl with crumbled bread for Silas. Then she went round to feed her other pets.

April had a magpie, a box with a harvest mouse in it, and two wild rabbits, who never got used to her and kicked and ran against the hutch until their noses bled whenever they saw her coming. They'd better watch it, or they'd go in a pie. There was a cage full of goldfinches. Little birds came and went regularly. April was expert at catching them. She used to have a rat but her mother sneaked out one night and let it go. She also had a grass snake she kept hidden in a wooden box in the long grass round the side of the house, because her mother would let that go, too, if she found it. All these pets needed their own breakfasts and April spent an hour every morning cleaning them out and feeding them. She shook seed into the finches' cage, with maybe a teasel head for a treat. The magpie would eat everything. He loved eggs most of all but she never gave him them in case he got free and stole eggs from other, smaller birds.

As she turned over rocks and dug in the sandpit for worms and beetles for her snake, April kept thinking of the new family she had seen last night. She was intensely curious about anything new. She could see the house from her garden and kept glancing across to see if the smoke was rising from the chimney yet. The house was the only one left of a row of three and to one side were the ragged bricks and rubble where the others had been pulled down. The one remaining stuck up like a fat finger on the edge of the village in front of a group of ash trees.

The new family lay in bed for hours. Overcome with curiosity, April finally crept over to the ash trees and climbed up the nearest one so she could spy in the window at the back. She could see the boy lying in bed. He looked very pale and thin and serious. He was awake; she could see his big dark eyes staring at the ceiling or the walls. April wanted to yell out to him, 'Good morning!' But she remembered his terrified look at her yesterday when she called and she slid quietly to the ground instead.

In the end she got bored waiting for something to happen and went off on her own as usual. Today April had the morning to be out and about in. It was a lovely morning, silky and cool with mist and the sun slowly coming through. The tide was pushing up the estuary. Sometimes April got into her boat and let the sea push her up the river right upstream as far as Cluinworth, where the Station Master would let her put the boat in the guard's wagon and ride with it back home. Today she was too full of energy. She crept out of the house and made sure no one was looking before she ran as fast as she could upstream. She slowed down when she was sure she was alone and walked up past the finger of woods by the riverside, up to the farm buildings below Ham Hill where the swallows nested.

A couple of hours later when she got back, the first thing she looked at was the stubby house on the edge of town. The smoke was thick from the chimney pot and a strong smell of fish was coming on the wind. April was curious but hungry. She went indoors for a second breakfast. As she ate it the fishy smell got stronger and stronger, until it was not so much fishy as gluey. April was delighted – something to investigate! She wanted a present by way of introduction. There were still two eggs left. Two seemed a bit mean, so she made up the numbers with two false ones her mother sometimes put under the broody hens. She popped the eggs into a paper bag and ran across.

April went the back way but she stopped short when she came suddenly upon the boy. He was beating a tree with a stick. He dropped the stick when he saw April. She took two steps backwards and glanced around. He was smaller than her and seemed to be alone. Still, she wasn't taking any chances. She dashed quickly over to the back door which was open and ran in, her anxious face glancing over her shoulder.

Tony followed her into the kitchen.

She stood by the stove. She was terrified. He didn't recognise her as the ghastly shouter from the day before. Then she had been covered in a towel and mud, but now she was wearing a printed frock and a short jacket over her shoulders.

'Did you want to speak to my mother? She's just popped out for a minute,' he said. The girl watched his face intensely. Her eyes flashed when he said that. Her face was so alive, it showed everything she thought and felt. He was between her and the door. She held out the packet of eggs to him. Tony reached across and took them.

'Oh. Are they for us?' She didn't seem to understand so he pointed at himself. 'For us?' April nodded. 'It's very kind of you.' He smiled politely and put them on the table. 'Are you going to wait? Would you like a cup of tea? The kettle's hot . . .' There was a pause. Tony nodded enquiringly at the kettle.

Reassured, April nodded. Tony went to put the kettle on and she began to move around the room, picking things up and looking at them and banging them down. He leaned against the table, embarrassed. Why wouldn't she speak? She didn't seem to mind she was in someone else's house but nosed about making a terrible noise, banging things about as if she didn't care. Yet she gave no sign that she knew she was making so much noise. The fish head was smelling terribly and Tony wanted to go back outside, but he didn't care to leave her on her own.

The tea was in the pot when his mother came in. She had a basket over her arm filled with fir cones for the fire.

'Oh, a visitor, how lovely,' she cooed, glancing suspiciously at the pot stinking on the stove. April grinned. She seized the eggs off the table and thrust them into the woman's hands.

'For us? Why, thank you. Look, Tony – fresh eggs. From your own chickens, I expect?'

April nodded enthusiastically. Barbara glanced at Tony. 'Thank you very much,' he said obediently. April nodded.

Barbara Piggot looked curiously at her. 'What's your name, my dear?'

April didn't try to answer. She shook her head and pointed to her mouth and then to her ears.

'Oh, I see. You can't . . . speak? Or hear?'

She smiled kindly at the girl. Tony stared sulkily, remembering that bawling from the window yesterday. He would not forgive her for drawing attention to him in that way.

All the time she talked, Barbara kept glancing at the pot bubbling on the cooker by the wall. Now she couldn't stand it any longer. 'Tony, it smells disgusting. Not soupy at all. I'm sure Mrs Parnell never made a smell like this.' She peered distastefully into the pot. The head had turned into a sticky, eyeless monster.

'I had to go outside to get away from it,' Tony complained.

'Didn't it occur to you to take it off?' she snapped.

'I told you, I don't know how to cook.'

'What shall we do, then, eat grass?' His mother was

19

almost yelling in anger, but she kept her head down so that the deaf girl, who could evidently lip read, wouldn't see the rage in her mouth. When she looked up she seemed as sweet as cream. 'We seem to have made a bit of a mess of our soup,' she told April.

April glanced from one to the other. Something was wrong. She went over to investigate the foul pot on the cooker. Inside was a disintegrating fish head. What on earth could they be doing with it? It was boiled to a pulp, burned, and a sticky half inch of yellow liquid glugged dismally at the bottom of the pan.

Barbara went over to the table. 'Soup's off,' she muttered, glaring at Tony, who looked blandly away. 'We have another one, we can try again, I suppose.'

'Oh, Mother, not again, it's awful,' complained Tony.

April turned suddenly and beamed at them. She started to chuckle. She'd had an idea. She seized the shopping list off the table and dipped one end of it into the yellow goo in the pan. She blew on it and then with a flourish stuck it on the wall. She pointed excitedly and made a noise that sounded like hooting to draw attention to her trick.

'Well! Look, Tony . . . We seem to have made a very effective . . . glue!' Despite herself Barbara began to giggle. Tony looked in amazement at the piece of paper on the wall and glanced shyly at his mother, who burst out laughing. April danced for joy that they liked her joke and began rushing around the room finding bits of paper and things to stick to the walls. Barbara walked over to pull off a piece of paper. It tore. Everyone was howling. Tony was getting hysterical, yelling, 'Soup! Soup! Who wants soup?' and April was sticking up anything she could lay her hands on. The glue was so strong it could hold up sticks and little stones. 'I'll have to clean it all off!' realised Barbara. Tony was screaming with laughter and April was hooting like a goose but Barbara felt exhausted and the laughter died suddenly in her. April was splashing stinking fish glue everywhere but Barbara couldn't be bothered to stop it. At least it was cheering Tony up, who was getting on her nerves with his sulks, but there was still the problem of lunch. Barbara glanced at the four eggs lying on the table.

'Scrambled eggs,' she thought. Barbara wasn't sure how you made scrambled eggs but she knew you had to break them, so she picked one up and tapped it on the edge of a saucepan. The saucepan rang. She frowned and tried again. April began to creep round to the door. Barbara gave the egg a good hard crack on the table. It was as solid as a rock.

'You like jokes, don't you?' she snapped.

April stared at her.

'I said, you like jokes. Bloody jokes!' screamed Barbara, and she lost control for the first time since she'd discovered her husband had left her with her boy and nothing else the day before. She screamed and flung the egg at the stone floor, where it cracked and rolled under the table. 'Jokes, jokes, bloody, bloody jokes!' she screamed at the startled girl. April turned and fled. Barbara picked up another egg and flung it after her. But this egg was real. It splattered violently on the door frame, covering the walls, the floor and the ceiling with wet.

'Oh . . .!' Barbara put her hand to her mouth and stared at the mess. Everything was suddenly very quiet. She glanced at her son, who was wedged in the corner staring at her. She closed her eyes and walked backwards to sit on the table.

'Go and find her, darling,' she said quietly, her hand

21

still glued to her mouth, her eyes shut. 'Tell her I'm sorry. Say, "Mrs Piggot apologises." Please go at once.'

Tony had no wish to go out onto the street; apart from anything else, people for miles around must have heard his mother's screaming. But he thought she was about to burst into tears so he ran out of the door after April.

April was standing at the end of the lane, where it faded into grass and brambles. She turned and ran when she saw him coming. Tony glanced around; no one else was about. He took a few steps after her but when he saw her glance over her shoulder, he stopped. She stopped too, and half hid herself behind a tree.

'Sorry!' mouthed Tony elaborately. 'Mother says sorry. She didn't mean it.' He smiled again and spread his hands. 'She says, "Mrs Piggot apologises." She's had a lot on her mind.' April stepped out from behind her tree. She stared at him very closely.

'Sorry!' repeated Tony cheerfully. April nodded. Tony nodded. He smiled and walked back to the house slowly. She watched him until he disappeared behind the building. She began to follow him but something – perhaps a faint whisper of the bell tolling – made her glance at the village clock. She almost jumped in her fright. Twelve – already so late. In a panic, April ran for home.

3

At twelve o'clock on Saturday everything in Cibblesham closed. All the shops, the fish packaging plant, the workshops, the woodyard. As April slammed the front door the hooter from the boatyard cried out from the other side of the village. The men and apprentices would down tools and make for home or maybe loiter along the river banks. Until her mother came back on Sunday afternoon, April was a prisoner.

The streets were almost certainly safe for the time being, full of people on the way home, but April felt better indoors until the lunch-hour was over. She sometimes felt that just to see her persecutors was as bad as what they did to her. The doors were locked, the windows were locked. There was food and she could have easily stayed inside the whole time but the trouble was she got so bored. What she wanted to do was run off down river, fish, boat, swim, play. That was unthinkable, of course. But she had friends. Saturday afternoons had become her time for visiting in the village.

In between her house and the village was a stretch of empty lane that curved out of sight of the rest of the village. April was so nervous about walking there alone that she waited for a train to come into the station and walked with the passengers round the blind curve into the safety of the houses. Once on the main street, she ran straight round to a little house with a conifer in a tub outside, where old Mrs Craddock lived.

Mrs Craddock expected her at this hour and always had some little cakes or scones and a pot of tea ready. April ate, Mrs Craddock gossiped. The old lady mouthed her words elaborately to start off with but soon forgot and just chatted away. April could follow her if she wanted to but often she just sat and smiled or frowned or looked surprised at what seemed like the right places. She nodded vigorously whenever the old lady mentioned someone she really wanted to hear about. Mrs Craddock seemed to know everything. In this way, the two passed an enjoyable hour or so.

After Mrs Craddock April usually called on Albert and Sheila Giles, who lived just round the corner. If Mrs Giles was there she might make a little conversation; she was one of the few people who could understand what April said, which was nice. But what April really hoped for was that Sheila would be busy. Then Albert, who was uncomfortable with the girl he couldn't talk to, led her into the front room where a huge shiny brown radio stood on a low table.

'I know what you want.' He winked. It amused him that she liked the radio so much even though she couldn't hear it. In fact, when he turned it on loud she could make out the trumping of the bass notes. She turned the tone towards the bass and lay against it and felt the deep, rich voice of the radio rumble in her chest and tried to follow the tune with her hollow voice.

There were one or two other people April could visit, but not many. Most of the village regarded her as a halfwit. That suited April. They left her alone. It had been all right when she was small but now there was a danger she could become trapped in her own myth.

Today April finished off her visiting by calling on her friend Jenny. They'd spent a lot of time together when they were small. When they got older and Jenny went to school they saw less of each other but they were still friends. It disturbed April to see her friend embarking on a life of school, work and family that seemed to be beyond her, but she liked Jenny and liked to keep in touch. Jenny could understand her speech and knew how to talk slowly and clearly. Today, Jenny was excited about a date that evening with Tad Main, an apprentice at the boatyard.

April couldn't help pulling a face.

'I know he's a bit rough but he treats me like china, really,' explained Jenny, a small-boned, pretty girl. 'He makes me feel . . . special,' she said, wrinkling her nose in amusement.

'Uh,' remarked April.

Jenny combed her long, fair hair with her fingers and looked at April. 'Don't you ever think about boys and that sort of thing?' she asked curiously. 'Would you like a boyfriend? My mum and dad say I'm too young, but I don't.'

April, who was pretty and could look very well if she cared to, had a way of making herself look like a surprised ape-girl, by hunching her back and shoulders.

'Ay?' she said, saying, 'Me?'

'Oh, don't be silly, I know you better than that,' said Jenny. 'I mean, what do you think of Tad? Would you go out with him? My father doesn't like him even though he's got a good job.'

But April wouldn't talk about Tad, or boys. Jenny got impatient and the two girls parted feeling cross.

April walked back to her house with Mrs Williams, who was catching the train to visit her son's family. When she got to the gate, the deaf girl ran fast to the kennel and untied Silas. He usually slept outside but at weekends she felt he was unsafe, as she was, and put him in the kitchen. He made a terrible mess, she'd have to scrub the floor before her mother came back but it was worth any kind of effort to keep her swan safe.

April, cunning and stubborn, had for years managed to avoid doing anything to help her mother. But on Saturday nights lately, too terrified to go out into the dark, she became so mad with boredom that she actually started to do the housework. Just to keep her hands busy she dusted and washed and scrubbed – the china, the dishes, the furniture, even the walls sometimes. She went over the patch of carpet in the living room with a soapy brush and was amazed at the colours that emerged. One Saturday she had dusted the coal lying in the fireplace ready for a cool night, and amused herself so much she ended up polishing it. Her mother was amazed when she lit the fire two nights later.

'Heavens, what coal . . . I never noticed the shine on it when I laid the fire. It's almost too good to burn.' April was beside herself with laughter but never let on, even when the burning coal filled the house with the smell of polish.

Her mother was delighted and surprised at this new development. She took it as a sign that April was growing up and it gave her hope that one day her strange child would live a normal life.

Tonight, after boiling some potatoes for her dinner, which she ate on their own with salt, and after doing the usual round of dusting, polishing and sweeping, April settled on the task of shining the windows and cleaning the curtains. The windows were easy – you doused them in soapy water and then polished them up with newspapers. She'd seen her mother do that. But she was too lazy to take the curtains down so she decided to sponge them and rub them still hanging.

She did one side okay. The colours looked brighter,

but whether this was from the wet or because of the dirt she'd taken off she couldn't say. They hadn't transformed as magically as the carpets, certainly. Now she was working on the other side. She had one foot on the mantelpiece and one on the back of an armchair. There was a bowl of water resting, like her, half on the sill and half on the chair, and April was sponging the curtain vigorously.

There was a noise under her. April looked down. At her feet was an ugly yellow face twisted out of shape, its lips stretched in a crude grin. It lay almost on its side. It was right on top of her foot gibbering silently and staring pop-eyed up her skirt.

April screamed. They were here now with her, in her house! She forgot everything, she clutched her skirt, flung out her arms . . . the bowl of water went flying and she crashed down, landing on her shoulder and jarring the wind out of her. She cringed, expecting them to jump on her. Her shoulder hurt horribly, as if she'd knocked it out of joint, and the pain made her feel sick and she was unable to breathe for a second. She grovelled backwards on the floor before they got on top of her.

Outside in the dark garden there was laughter but April heard nothing. She still half believed they were in the house with her. They could be hiding behind the settee, outside, up the chimney, anywhere. Her eyes swivelled madly about the room trying to work out where they were. She leaned against an armchair, clutching her aching shoulder and snatching for breath. The face again appeared, leering suddenly in the light from the room. It was Joe Hoggins, the postmaster's son. His mouth moved at her.

April screamed. She jumped up and pulled the wet curtains and ran upstairs, slamming the doors behind her. Surely they wouldn't dare . . .? But already they were in the garden! Her heart pounding, she ran into her room where she fell by the side of her bed. She pulled the covers on top of her and waited for the floor to shake under her as they came pounding up after her. But the floor was still.

After several minutes April crept up and peered out of the window, hiding behind the curtains. At the gate was a figure. Tad Main, Jenny's new boyfriend. Now Joe came out of the garden to join him. She wanted to scream in rage at them for scaring her but she didn't dare.

They turned away, laughing, and walked back to the village. Tad would be on his way to pick up Jenny for their date. April collapsed on the floor and wept. They scared her so much, deep, deep inside. She knew what they were after and she was all alone.

When she recovered, April ran to the cupboard in the hall and took out a large woollen blanket. She collected a bottle of water from the kitchen, slipping and sliding on Silas's droppings in her hurry. She tore off a few chunks of bread and a lump of cheese. She had to hurry, she was certain that now they had come right up to the windows they'd soon be inside, here, with her. She locked Silas hissing in the pantry. She ran around the house and drew all the curtains. Then she ran as fast as she could down to the jetty. She didn't have long. Tad was off but Joe might come back any time if he didn't find something else to amuse him.

She kept fumbling the knot to her mooring and almost fell into the little boat. As soon as it steadied itself she pushed off into the darkness. She felt safe on the water. But then she had felt safe in her house. Lately the boys had grown so large in her fears that they seemed capable of anything.

It had started years ago when they were all small and played together. Sometimes the boys had bribed her with sweets to show them what she'd got. April didn't care . . . why shouldn't they see if they wanted to? The other girls had done it too. April had played that game longer than the others, just because it was bad. Later on the big boys dropped the younger boys. Then, if they caught April on her own, they'd catch her and touch her up. April hated it, although they tickled her to make her laugh. It was later on when they left school and got their apprenticeships at the boatyard that Tad, Joe and sometimes one or two of the other boys got really bad. They took to lying in wait for her and jumped her. They were rough. They held her down by sitting on her arms and legs and didn't seem to care that it hurt her, while they took it in turns at running their hands on her bare skin under her clothes, and pinched and poked her. They always tickled her, as if her frantic squeals of laughter meant she was enjoying it.

As time went by they got bolder and stronger. Now they'd taken to stripping her and poking her with straws and sticks, or rubbing their new moustaches on her breasts. If she struggled or fought back they became cruel. At weekends when her mother was away, she was theirs if they could find her. The more they did to her the crueller they became, as if she was some charm who made them worse every time they touched her. This was why the sight of Tony scared her; this was why she never dared leave the house in the evenings and imprisoned herself at weekends. April lived in terror of those boys.

29

Every time it got worse. She was certain that if they caught her again they would rape her.

April dipped the oars quietly in the water, skimming downstream. Further on, closer to the estuary, the river was filled with little islands. April knew them all, and one in particular was her secret. She was safe there – safer now than in her own home. From now on she would sleep out on Friday and Saturday nights.

She pulled hard against the current. She didn't know it but the boys were very near. Joe had met a friend and the two had gone to the off-sales at the pub, where the landlord would sell them bottles of beer. They had carried their beer away to drink by the boatyard. Sitting on the boatmaker's quay, Joe and his friend heard the quiet chop of her oars in the water, and speculated that a big fish might have risen out there. They looked for stones to throw, but there were none.

It was late May but a cold night. April slept little. She didn't dare light a fire. She imagined the boys would follow her, and where would her hideaway be then? She had a store of things hidden away, wrapped in a tarpaulin in the thickets. She set out a few fish lines, ate her supper of bread and cheese and then crept away into the thickets to try and sleep. She pulled the blanket around her but the cold ground crept into her bones. Soon she got up and went round her lines. Nothing yet. Now it was getting damp with dew as well as cold. Pulling her blanket round her shoulders, April began a steady, noisy tramp round and round the island, disturbing ducks roosting at the water's edge, song birds in the little branches of trees, pigeons higher up, until there wasn't a living thing asleep on her small kingdom.

Dawn came at five o'clock, by which time April had been round the island maybe fifty times. She checked her lines again and pulled in a flounder as long as her shin, which she would have for her breakfast at home. As the sun came up the birds began to sing. April paused to watch the sun come up above the mist as the birdsong swelled enormously around her. The island was filled to overflowing with tiny, invisible birds, singing their hearts out. But in April's world there was no birdsong. All she knew of it were the vibrations she felt in the breasts of little birds she caught and held in her fist.

Soon, she tidied up her camp, dumped her provisions back in her boat and set off home.

She came back with the tide as it pushed the river back upstream, past the sleeping pastures, the hedgerows, the woodlands and villages. Wrapped up in her blanket in the bottom of the boat, April fell asleep in the cool sunshine and when she woke, the sun was high. She was stuck in a reed bed some half mile past Cibblesham. April estimated eight o'clock. She snatched the oars and began to row back in a panic. The boys would be up and about already.

Uncle Bob turned up at nine o'clock on Sunday morning, earlier than expected because he had some people to visit that day for lunch. When the long shiny black car pulled up outside the tiny cottage, Tony felt both ashamed that it should draw attention to them and proud because everyone could see the sort of people he and his mother really were.

Uncle Bob rubbed Tony's hair and said, 'Run along and play, there's a lad. Your mother and I have to have a talk.'

Tony glanced at his mother, who nodded. 'Thank you,'

he said. He walked along the road towards the river which he still hadn't explored. The church bells were ringing, peal after peal chiming in the still air.

Although his mother said they shouldn't depend on Uncle Bob, Tony had high hopes. Uncle Bob was rich, richer than his father. Now that his father had gone, surely it was his uncle's responsibility to keep them? He wouldn't expect them to remain where they were.

There was no one else. His mother's family had been very wealthy indeed and she had grown up in an enormous house with dozens of servants. But they had lost all their money years ago. Since then her father and mother had died and her brother had left for Canada, where no one had heard of him for years. His mother had countless friends and Tony had spent weekends in some of their large country houses. But these people would not offer them more than holidays. Nobody wanted to find themselves with a couple of paupers on their hands. Uncle Bob was their only hope.

Tony crept quickly past the station house in case the mad girl spotted him again. Then he walked over the railway footbridge and down by a woodyard to the river. The tide was in, the water full and inviting, nestling right up to the grasses and bushes growing on the banks. All the horrid mud he had seen on the journey here had gone. Tony felt tired and dirty. He would have liked a swim. Perhaps Uncle Bob would take them away at once and he would get a hot bath, wrap up in huge fluffy new towels and sleep in a proper bed tonight. Wanting to make a good impression on his uncle, Tony dipped his hands in the water and rubbed his face vigorously to get it clean. Then he combed his hair.

He hung around near the railway bridge so that he

could keep an eye on the house. His uncle was there for about an hour. As soon as he saw him emerge he ran as fast as he could to catch him. Bob saw the boy running up the road towards him and paused, his hands in his pockets. He leaned awkwardly on the wing of his Bentley.

'Uncle Bob...' As he ran, Tony began to panic. It looked as though his uncle was going to leave without them and the thought of being abandoned in this terrible hole scared him silly. He began shouting long before he got there and was out of breath by the time he arrived. His mother was watching him with a face like fury. He thought she was cross with his manners.

'Sorry, sir,' he said, and then blushed, because he never called his uncle 'sir' usually.

'Hello, Tony!' said his uncle cheerily. He reached out and rubbed the boy's hair again and winked.

'Are we going to have to live here long, Uncle?' begged Tony. 'I-I – want to know when I'll be starting school again, you see.'

His uncle looked down at the earnest face staring up at him. He pursed his lips, glanced at Barbara, and winked again. 'We'll get you out of here in no time, old son. You'll see!' He reached in his pocket and gave Tony a half-crown. 'In no time!' he repeated. He climbed into the car.

It was going to be all right! 'Thank you, sir, thank you, thank you!' cried Tony, overcome with joy because his uncle was getting them out. 'Thank you, thank you... Mother and I have been so worried...' He began to gambol round and round the car like an idiot as his heroic uncle waved his hand, blew a kiss at his mother and pulled away. He blew the horn as he drove off. Tony chased the car a few yards and then stood waving until he was out of sight. He glanced anxiously at his mother who stood quietly in the doorway. He ran back and followed her into the kitchen.

'When are we moving? Have you arranged something? Is it all set up?' he demanded.

Barbara Piggot brushed a wisp of hair from her face. She looked unexpectedly wan and tired. She went to put the kettle on the hob and gave her son an odd, curious glance.

'Uncle Bob has offered us . . . the possibility of a house in Colchester. A little town place . . . not what we were used to. Better than this.'

'Will I be going back to St. Robin's? Or another school? Did you discuss my education?' demanded Tony.

'Not exactly.'

'I don't care, I hated Robs, anyway. When are we going?'

Tony's mother rubbed the edge of her finger across her lip and watched Tony thoughtfully. She had no idea what sort of a person her son was. When he was small a nanny had cared for him; then there had been boarding school. In the holidays they sometimes had days out, but these were always curiously formal affairs. There was so little personal to them.

But it was different now. He deserved some sort of explanation.

'I told him I'd have to think about it,' she said at last.

'What about?' He stared around in alarm. 'Isn't it enough? Do you think you can get something better out of him?'

'Oh no, no. Not that.' Mrs Piggot got up and went to take the kettle off the hob as it came to the boil. 'There is a bit of a catch. Your uncle wants me and him . . . to live together. As man and wife.'

'But you're already married.' Tony frowned. 'Is Father dead?'

'No, no. Alive and kicking, by all accounts.'

'He wants you to get a divorce?' Tony scowled, unable to make it out. 'Does he . . . love you?'

'I don't think that's what he has in mind.'

'I don't understand . . .'

Mrs Piggot rubbed her face and looked up at the ceiling. Her boy would have to grow up quickly. 'Uncle Bob wants me to be his mistress, darling,' she explained in a clear voice.

Tony froze. His mother? Saying this to him . . .? This smutty talk. Women who talked like that were . . . no good.

'Mmmmm . . .' he began to say the word but was too embarrassed to finish. He wondered if she was teasing him. She was always teasing. It didn't seem like it. 'Uncle Bob,' he began, but he couldn't go on. He was about to say that Uncle Bob was a nice man. He had even given him half a crown. He could feel it in his pocket, the weight of the big coin on his leg.

'Actually I'm not sure mistress is the right word,' she continued, walking up and down the narrow aisle between the table and the stove. 'To be a mistress you're supposed to love, or at least like the man and I'm not really very fond of Bob.' She glanced at her son to see if he was taking all this in. It was none of his business, really. But she was angry. 'There's another word to describe women who do such things purely for the financial arrangements, isn't there?' she said. She looked again at him and smiled. 'Do they teach you such things at school?'

Horrified with embarrassment, Tony looked away.

'You needn't be so surprised,' she went on. She continued pacing rapidly up and down, not looking at him. Now that she'd begun she was determined that he should know everything – everything. There was no room for secrets any more. 'It's not such an uncommon arrangement. A great many men keep mistresses. My father for one. Not to mention your father.'

Tony watched her out of the corner of his eye. He wished he could turn to stone and be insensible to what was happening to him. Outside the cheerful church bells started up again. His mother was relentlessly pulling his world all to pieces.

'Funny thought for you, I expect,' said his mother. 'Sorry.'

Tony looked at her sideways and said, 'Didn't you mind?'

'Well of course I did, terribly. But I got used to it. The trouble is that your father broke the rules and fell in love and ran away with the girl. Which is terribly inconsiderate of him.'

Tony suddenly wanted to hit her. 'You couldn't keep him,' he hissed.

'No.' She rubbed her nose. 'I could have left him, though – a great many times. I had plenty of offers. But there is supposed to be a degree of loyalty in marriage, you see. To the children apart from anything else.'

Barbara regretted saying that as soon as it left her lips, and she silently winced and put her hand to her mouth. Tony knew. His father hadn't just left his mother; he'd left Tony, too.

'He's taken a house in Ballad Street, apparently, he and his girl,' said his mother, watching her son's still face. Ballad Street was a few roads away from where they used to live. She turned suddenly to hide her own face. It made her sick to think of this floosy sleeping in her bed, sitting on her chairs. Bob had made great play of the details, as if making her angry at her husband would make her more likely to submit. There had always been rivalry between the two men. No doubt this was a way to get back at his older brother.

Barbara tapped her teeth anxiously. 'I wonder if the bank knows about all this . . .'

'What are you going to do?' asked Tony.

She raised her eyebrows and sighed. 'I'm not terribly sure that I care to be Uncle Bob's mistress,' she announced thoughtfully. 'What do you think, darling?'

Tony could only shake his head.

'I'm so glad you agree.' She looked carefully at him. He was dumbstruck. . . dumbstruck with the realisation that everything had been different from the way it seemed, dumbstruck with embarrassment that his mother was speaking about her private life with him. 'I'm so sorry, darling. I did warn you not to rely on Uncle Bob.'

'But what are we going to do . . .' Tony sat down at the table. As he spoke he began to weep. It was all different and it had always been different. His mother came to sit next to him in a business-like manner. She put her arm round him and her face close to his. He could smell her perfume, the musky, clean smell of her.

'I have a few more tricks up my sleeve. I told you . . . I have all sorts of wonderful talents you couldn't even guess. Why, I can speak French, Italian, German. I can sing like a lark, play the piano. There'll be people queuing up for me to teach them. We'll make pots of money. And I have a few letters to write. Friends, connections . . . you'll see. In the meantime, we have to be brave and resourceful.'

37

Tony tried to control his traitorous face. 'Aren't we getting any money at all, then?' he asked.

'Your father has granted us an allowance, apart from paying the rent here. Ten pounds a month. I spend that much on clothes.' Tony glanced up at the sound of her voice. Her face had become hard and ugly with rage for a moment. Then she shrugged and went on. 'It's in the post apparently. Uncle Bob has promised to help. He said he'd send something along.'

Tony looked at her. She winked.

'I haven't said no, yet, you see. Sometimes we have to be a little cunning.' She smiled prettily. 'He'll keep paying us something for a little longer. Until we learn how to earn something for ourselves. We can do better than this place, you and me, once we put our minds to it. I would guess that Uncle Bob thinks that a few weeks of poverty will grind us down. But he'll find out otherwise – won't he, darling?'

Tony looked away. How he hated her!

'We'll have to do whatever we can to keep your poor old mother off the streets!' She chuckled and kissed his cheek. She was as pretty as a picture as she always managed to be. Everytime he looked at her she seemed to be just visiting this dingy hovel they lived in. But Tony was so livid with rage because she had broken silence on the truth that he turned his head from her and wouldn't speak.

'Come on!' She stood up briskly and went to straighten herself up in the mirror. 'Time for church. Hear the bells!'

'You don't normally go to church,' said Tony looking at her.

'I never felt the need before,' observed Barbara. 'In these circumstances, it's a good idea to be seen to be

38

decent, do you see? Besides,' she added, turning back to the mirror and patting her hair into place, 'it's a good way to meet people. We're going to need people.'

4

Until her mother came back at midday, Sunday was another day of fear for April. But there was one safe place. For the first time in her life April had taken to church going. She sat in a pew with the rest of them, watching the vicar's mouth open and silently close and feeling the organ rumble in her ears and stomach, kicking her heels on the woodwork, or noisily sucking her fingers to the irritation of the other churchgoers. By the time she got home, her mother would usually be back and there would be a delighted reunion as she ran round the house inspecting the glories of April's housework.

On this Sunday, April's mind was full of the new people who made glue out of fish heads and threw tantrums and had such lovely manners. She was sure they would go to church. They had spoken to her as if she were a real person. 'Sorry,' he had said. And, 'Thank you very much.' Not only that but, 'Mrs Piggot apologises.' These were all phrases April knew very well indeed, but no one ever said them to her. The last phrase especially delighted her. 'Mrs Piggot apologises . . .' She'd repeated it over and over while she did the housework and during her long cold night on the island, laughing to herself and wondering where such manners came from. The boy and his mother were tall and pale as if they weren't used to life. They were funny. April wanted to be friends. In her secret heart of hearts, although she never dared think it, she wanted to be like them.

About twenty minutes before the service was due to start, in the middle of cleaning up the pantry after Silas, April suddenly decided she was going to make a splash.

The vicar was always telling her to dress smartly for church. She usually ignored him but this time she would do it. But smart was not nearly good enough for April. Her mother had bought her all sorts of slacks and dresses and cardigans and skirts, sensible wear that April disdained. She didn't even bother to look in her wardrobe.

She went to her mother's wardrobe and selected a dress – a long, slinky dress with a low neck-line and no sleeves. She found a hat that her mother wore with it and the right high-heeled shoes. She peeled her own dress over her head, and looked at herself in the mirror. In honour of church, today she would wear a bra! Her own, which she hated, was a heavy contraption of flesh coloured cotton and bone. None of her mother's fitted, but the bright white underwear seemed more suitable. Stockings, too. She wasted minutes on the suspender belt and it felt awful; she kept snatching at her thighs from the feeling that the stockings were falling down. Then for the make-up. April was inexperienced but she had a steady, clever hand and made a good job of it. She stood in front of the mirror surveying herself. She looked . . . rather good.

April giggled at the thought of how surprised everyone would be when they saw her dressed up like a day at the races!

But the splash still wasn't big enough. Now April had her great inspiration. She ran to her room and from a drawer took out a handsome black leather dog collar with dull silver studs all the way round it. Her dog, Barkus, used to wear it for best. Barkus had died two years ago and April hadn't felt like trying to replace the dear old thing but she'd kept the collar. She polished up the studs and ran down to where Silas was sitting outside his kennel. This would show them!

41

The collar didn't fit properly and April had to bore a hole in it with a skewer. Once she got it on, Silas looked wonderful . . . his snowy white feathers and his bright orange bill contrasting wonderfully with the dark leather of the collar. He arched his wings and dipped his head, as if he knew he was required to be especially handsome today.

And now April was ready for church. With her hat tipped back on her head, the cool air on her arms and breast and her heart singing inside her with excitement, she led Silas out of the garden gate and up the road to St. James'.

They had to go slowly. Silas waddled along like a fat old lady, stopping here and there to peck at some green stuff growing out of the cracks in the pavement and walls, or squirting his droppings on the road. By the time they got to the church the service had already started and the congregation was singing a hymn. April adjusted her suspenders and hat. She stood for a second in the shadow behind the door, breathing in the familiar church smell of musty wood. Then she pushed the door open and led Silas inside.

The effect was superb. Heads turned, faces were pulled. The organ, which entered April's world through the deep notes that boomed in her ears and rumbled through her stomach, faltered; the singing became confused with laughter and whispers. April held her head high and made her way down the centre aisle. She could see the new people staring in awe at her and she felt so proud, so proud. Her swan would certainly add something to the worship today. Probably the vicar would ask her to bring him every Sunday! She caught sight of Tad and Joe sitting together sniggering at her. April lifted her nose in the air, turned her shoulders away from them and paced grandly forward.

Now the vicar came hurriedly down from the lectern towards her. Convinced he was coming to congratulate her, April paused and beamed at him.

'No swans,' said the vicar firmly.

April scowled.

'No pets,' explained the vicar, pointing and shaking his head. He was trying to look neither amused nor cross, even though he was both.

April looked round. It was true. Hers was the only pet in here. She had never noticed before, but it was certainly true. She couldn't for the life of her think why, though.

The vicar was trying not to roll his eyes in despair. Why on earth couldn't the girl ever get it right? The dress was almost off her shoulder! And make-up – bright red lipstick in church! Sometimes he thought there was more going on in that head than April liked to let out, but at times like this he was certain that it was as everyone said. The girl was not only deaf, but an idiot and a malicious one at that. He felt a nut of anger swell in him.

'Tie him up outside and come back in,' he mouthed at her. But April had already decided that if God didn't want Silas, He wasn't getting her either. She stuck her nose up at the vicar, and to the amusement of the congregation, turned round and stalked back out. She was about to go home in a sulk, but she still wanted to show off Silas to the new people. It struck her she could make a good impression sauntering in the churchyard as the congregation came out. So she led the swan about on his lead, letting him nibble at the grass between the graves, encouraging him to flap up onto the tombstones, as she waited for the service to end. Behind her the organ struck up. And from down the line, unheard by April, came the faint chuff-chuffing of the steam train carrying April's mother back to Cibblesham.

The train pulled in several minutes later and Mrs Dean hurried off into the village with her overnight bag.

'Morning, Helen,' called the guard. She waved and made her way to the house. April would be in church. That was something. But the way she dressed! All muddy legs and straw in her hair. And no bra! If only she could get her to wear that bra!

As she hurried up to the gate she saw that Silas was missing from his kennel by the door. She ran to the end of the garden, where she could see the church. Sure enough, there was the white shape of the swan and the figure of . . . was that her daughter? At first she thought it couldn't be, but then she recognised the dress. It was her best party dress, the one with the low front. At church!

With a miserable wail, Helen Dean dropped her bag and ran up the road to the churchyard. Her worst fears were coming true. The wretched girl was even wearing make-up, red lipstick – well put on too. She must have been practising. As she ran in the gate, Mrs Dean saw April hitch up her dress, revealing a lacy suspender belt and stocking with a black seam up the back. She leaned against a gravestone, in full view of the open church door, and scratched at the bare top of her thigh like a . . .

Mrs Dean ran straight up. April watched in surprise as she swung her hand with a crack on her daughter's face. 'You bloody little slut! What have you been up to?' Her mother hissed the words in a violent undertone,

44

caught between propriety and rage. But the rage was winning. She slapped again and again at her daughter's head. April groaned loudly. She grabbed her breasts to show she was wearing a bra like a good girl, but she almost popped out of the flimsy lace thing. Her mother was driving her up the path, shoving her in the back. It had happened! Stockings, make-up, boys, sex, everything she most feared had happened already. How long would it be before the girl was pregnant? How long would it be before the village worthies – the vicar, the doctor, the wealthy – decided that enough was enough and got her put away? Mrs Dean was not just angry for herself. It was so important that April learn to behave herself, but she didn't seem interested in even trying. Mrs Dean was desperate for her sake.

Behind them, a discreet hand closed the church door. 'You stupid, stupid girl, why don't you listen for once?' yelled Mrs Dean. 'Do you want to get taken away? Go on, get home, get home . . .'

April ran before her. Behind them in the churchyard, Silas, who was perched on the top of a grave, realised suddenly he was being abandoned. In a panic he leapt up and tried to fly after her, but his pinions were kept well trimmed and he spun in a long arc before crashing into the church wall. Picking himself up he began to hurry after the crying girl, running and falling on the gravel road.

It was awful, the whole village was awful, thought Tony. It was more awful than anything that that mad girl was trying to be friends with them and that her mother, who must be equally mad, was beating her up on the other side of the church door. They were so common.

And yet . . . April had made him laugh and feel better

the day before; and for maybe a minute when she appeared in the church door with her swan, she had transformed everything. Among all the stiff collars and neatly buttoned-up dresses, April had appeared like a spirit, a vision – the only living thing among them all. The vicar, the congregation, her mother had all made her ridiculous, but for that minute she had been wonderful.

As he heard her honking like a donkey on the road Tony felt humiliated and hated her all the more because she had affected him so deeply.

Despite all this, he felt sorry for her.

That night in bed, Tony lay and plotted against his mother. The things she had told him were wrong. They were secrets, unspoken things. It was smut that boys whispered to each other in secret. And yet she had told him it all with no apparent shame. It was a filthier thing to speak it than to do it. No wonder his father had left her! This new woman of his father's must be a prostitute or something. How shameful for his mother that his father should prefer a prostitute to her! That was her failure.

One of the sixth formers at his school used to visit prostitutes in the town and had been expelled. It was said that no less than two of the teachers had mistresses. But this was rumour and words. He remembered Talls, a boy in his year, who boasted that his father was having an affair. Talls was proud of the fact. He seemed to think his father was clever to do such a thing, but Talls was living at home and Tony was a beggar.

Obviously there was something wrong with his mother. That was why his father had left her. But why should Tony suffer with her? As he swore and raged in his heart, Tony saw a way he might get out of this on his own. He did not believe that his father would desert him. No doubt his weak, wicked mother had insisted on bringing him along.

Tony waited, coldly hating her as he lay still, until he heard his mother come up the stairs, heard the springs on her own bed creak and grow still. He waited still longer to be sure she was asleep before he got up quietly. He still had his school bag, one of the few things he now owned. He took out paper and pen and envelopes, lit the candle and began to write.

'Dear Father . . .'

He would be no bother. He stressed that. Most of the time he'd be at school. It might even be possible for him to spend some of the holidays with his friends, there was usually an invitation. If he did have to come home he would be on his best behaviour. His father and his – step-mother, he wrote after some thought – would hardly know he was there. Why, he would even be willing to spend the holidays with his mother, if no other arrangement was possible.

When it was done he sealed the envelope and wrote 'Mr Elliot Piggot, Ballad Street, Gildhamstead' on the front. He didn't know the number but he was sure the postman would know the name. The following morning first thing he took Uncle Bob's half-crown to the village Post Office and bought a stamp. He could expect a reply within a few days; he'd probably be home for the weekend, or back at school. He spent another three-pence on fruit cake at the baker's and went by the river on his own to eat it. He sat on the jetty and watched the ducks and swans gather round his feet for the crumbs. He fed them nearly the whole cake.

Barbara Piggot was an accomplished woman but with no money she was as helpless as a baby. Money did everything. It cooked her breakfast and washed her dishes. It brushed her hair, cleaned her clothes, lit her fire and allowed her to live the refined and civilised life she was used to. Money carried her between house, friends and theatre and stood like a loyal and silent slave between her and every drop of sweat, every spot of dirt the world cast up.

Barbara assumed . . . although she could not be sure . . . that Elliot did not intend keeping her in this condition forever. She knew exactly what the whole thing was about. Elliot had wanted a separation from her for years. There was no problem about that . . . neither of them could understand how it was that they had agreed to marry each other in the first place, because they had nothing in common. Barbara had told him years ago that if he wanted to leave he was welcome to go. The problem was, Elliot was simply not rich enough. When she married him she had believed his fortunes in the bank would continue up and up. But he seemed to get stuck somehow. He'd had no promotion for years and none seemed likely. If they split up now, there was only enough money to float one of them above the needs and cares of a harsh world. The other would suffer that worst of fates, poverty. There were no state benefits in 1925. You had what you earned or owned or stole, nothing more.

Elliot had made her various offers over the years but they had always fallen very far short of what Barbara expected. Every now and then he had blustered and threatened but she never took it seriously. She had underestimated him. Now he had taken matters into his own hands.

Barbara had been visiting friends in Hampshire when Elliot had made his move. She had come back to her house with no warning of what would be waiting for her. She stepped out of the taxi to find her house empty, boarded up and the locks changed. She stood helplessly on the front doorstep surrounded by her suitcases and boxes, furiously counting the few pounds in her purse until an embarrassed neighbour handed her an envelope containing a brief note from her husband. Her stubbornness had left him no choice, he said. He had left her for good. A taxi would be delivering Tony to Gildhamstead railway station the following morning and the boy would be bearing a letter to her containing instructions of how to get to their new house, together with her monthly allowance.

Barbara had spent the night with a friend and rung frantically around to try and trace her husband, with no success. It was just spiteful, of course, that when Tony handed over the letter the following morning there had been no money in it. Elliot wanted to be sure she knew just how deeply in his power she was.

This squalid little house, this miserable income was far, far less than anything he had offered before. Realistically he could hardly expect her to spend the rest of her days like a skivvy – could he? Barbara could see the scene at breakfast in the new household every morning. Elliot would be eyeing up the post . . . and eyeing up his little whore who no doubt would be prettily half dressed for the occasion . . . and wondering when the letter would arrive. The letter would be from Barbara. She would no doubt write in her usual elegant manner and hand but the content would be far from elegant. She would be not asking, but begging . . . begging him to relent and to rescue her and forgive her for her stubbornness. And, of course, begging him to allow her to accept any terms . . . any terms . . . he cared to offer her.

And if she didn't write such a letter? It made her sweat to think that the longer she left it, the more he might grow used to the idea that he really could leave her to rot in this hole. What Elliot had done was shameful, but it was not illegal. His were all the rights, his was all the power. Legally Barbara was more or less his possession. She might get a settlement through the court, but that could take months or even years.

Barbara felt that she would rather die than write such a letter. The trouble was, she would also rather die than suffer the shame and humiliation of having to earn a living and run a house with her own hands.

Of only one thing she was certain: if she had to go down in the world, she wasn't going to be helpless in it. She would do whatever she had to do and she would do her best to look cheerful about it, even though it poisoned her heart to do it.

She spent Monday morning on her knees trying to swab clean the kitchen floor with a torn sheet. Her knees hurt after a few minutes, so she tore the sheet in half and wrapped one half round her knees. When Tony came back he was desperate with shame and lurked out the back keeping watch to see that no one caught his mother in her filthy, sopping knee rags about such menial tasks. As if it wasn't bad enough that she was prepared to sink so low as to do such jobs, she made it worse by making tasteless jokes about it.

'I think I'd be better at being a mistress than a skivvy,'

she told him gaily. Tony was white with fury. All the time he was thinking of that letter, which would now be on the train on its way to Gildhamstead. Barbara herself was feeling guilty, very unsure that she had done the right thing in telling him the truth. It didn't seem to have helped him.

'You are a sulky boy this morning,' she told him lightly. Tony said nothing. It was impossible to talk about.

'I suppose you'd have preferred it if I had told you nothing and done what Uncle Bob wanted? Would that have been the decent thing?' she asked him, staring sideways up at him from the floor. Tony looked away and refused to answer.

Well, he was young, it was early days. Barbara tried to forget it and got on with her cleaning. She was doing her best to be bright for his sake but inside her was growing a tight knot of frustration and despair. At the end of an hour the floor was still flooded with filthy water and she felt crippled in her back and knees. The sausages that she'd put on for lunch had mysteriously turned inside out – she'd never seen sausages behave like it before. They ended up as an inedible crust stuck to the bottom of the frying pan. Nothing was working. The whole thing was so impossible and horrible that the only hope she could think of was that someone would gallop in the door and rescue them, although she had no idea who it could be. When the help finally did arrive it was from the last quarter she could imagine – from the deaf girl, April Dean.

April came round at about midday on Monday with more eggs to make up for her trick on Saturday. She knocked and pushed open the door and stared at the black water with its soapy grey froth that had gathered in a pond under the table.

'Good morning, dear,' smiled Barbara up from the floor. She waved her hand suavely about. 'I'm afraid it's a little wet underfoot today.' She was furious and filthy but she tried her best to look her usual elegant self. Just the effort made her suddenly see the funny side of it. She started to chuckle weakly, her head hanging between her elbows and her shoulders shaking.

April summed the whole thing up at a glance. She put the eggs down on the draining board and disappeared out of the door. She was back five minutes later with a mop and bucket which she shook at Barbara.

'Oh, of course,' exclaimed the helpless woman. 'I remember now . . . that's what one uses . . .'

April began energetically mopping down the floor. When all the water was gone she drew fresh from the tap and began all over again. She got through ten buckets and the water was still running brown. Barbara ran about exclaiming her delight, lifting the chairs onto the table under April's direction, sweeping up clusters of dust and dirt when the girl pointed them out. When all was done and the floor was gleaming and fresh, April set about the table. She cleared it and began to scrub. Barbara, who knew a good thing when she saw it, skipped about clapping her hands and couldn't thank the girl enough. Halfway through April stopped and handed her the scrubbing brush and she set to it as she had seen the girl doing, scrubbing the table free of all the sticky marks the last few dinners had left on it.

'Mother . . . let her do it,' hissed Tony when April was looking away.

'Don't be ridiculous, we can't expect her to skivvy for us for nothing. I'll just have to learn . . . and you. Look

52

at her ...' April was scraping away at the stove now. 'She's a gift from Heaven. Now you do the washing-up. And look like you love it!'

Tony snorted and went out to sulk in among the ash trees behind the house. Why should he lift a finger? He would be rescued in a few days, back at school ... wouldn't he? Of course, Tony wasn't so sure. Already, that letter was making him feel horrible. But he couldn't shake off the hope that it was all his mother's fault and that his father wanted him back after all.

'My dear, you have no idea how helpless I've been,' his mother told April when it was all done. 'I do hope you'll find the time to pop round again, until I get a bit more used to this sort of thing.'

Barbara spoke slowly, but her speech was unusual and much of it went over the girl's head. But the charm came over. April beamed.

'I'd love to ask you to stay for lunch, but ...' Barbara scraped with a knife at the frying pan and loosened a layer of black grease.

April stared at the object for a minute before she recognised it and said something that might have been 'au-age?' in her loud voice. Barbara admitted it and both she and the girl roared with laughter. Outside, Tony heard their laughter. He sneered and carried on digging in the earth with a stick.

As April cooked them a lunch of mashed potatoes, sausages and poached eggs, Barbara hung over her, following carefully how to do everything: how to peel the potatoes so that you didn't lose too much flesh, how to prick the sausages so they didn't burst, not to have the fire too hot. Tony was attracted back by the smell and got angry again because his mother was taking instructions in skivvying from a deaf idiot. But he didn't want to miss his meal, so he helped lay the table when he was asked, and watched hungrily as the sausages browned nicely.

'April, you've been an absolute godsend. I only wish there was some way we could repay you,' beamed Barbara as April served up. 'What do you think, Tony?' she turned anxiously to her son, who was staying as far removed from the whole thing as possible. 'There must be something we can do . . . something we can teach her in exchange . . .?'

'Singing lessons?' enquired Tony innocently, making sure that April's face was averted. 'French, German . . .?'

'Yes, and we don't exactly have a piano, do we?' said his mother, glancing anxiously at the girl, whose back was turned to the stove. 'Oh dear. I don't suppose her mother will be too keen on her becoming an unpaid maid to the down at heel . . .'

April wanted no reward. She was delighted that these people seemed to need her. She was not used to being needed; usually she got what she wanted by being helpless. She was even more delighted to be invited to join them for lunch. Here she was helping the aristocracy and sitting eating at the same table with them! But her new confidence did not last long. April tucked in as usual, using her fork like a scoop and bending low over her plate. Then she saw their faces and knew; her manners were letting her down. She scowled. She had for years refused to learn table manners, acting up the village image of her as a wild girl. But now she had become, suddenly and wonderfully, a useful and important person and she felt ashamed.

But Barbara affected delight. 'How wonderful! My dear, I've just realised how I can help you. Fair exchange . . . I was feeling so terribly awful that I had

54

no way of repaying you. Here . . .' She leaned across, took April's hands and arranged the cutlery in them. 'Did you know I was brought up in a big house with dozens of servants, like Lady Muck? You wouldn't think so now,' she laughed, although of course you would, 'but I still remember how we used to do things. Would you like it if I taught you how to behave like a proper lady? So that whenever you want to you can eat and dress and move about just like the King and Queen in Buckingham Palace do. Would you like that?' She beamed. April didn't seem so sure, so she added, 'And I expect it will come in handy when you have a family of your own. Why, you'll be able to teach your own children if you like! What do you say . . . do say yes, it will make us feel so much better, won't it, Tony?'

April stared back into her face as she talked, trying to work it all out. She didn't understand all of it. She knew Barbara wanted to teach her manners, like so many other people in the past; but this time it was different. Barbara paused and smiled. 'For when you have a family . . . a family,' she enunciated. 'When you have children.'

April stared down at her brown hands, enclosed in the soft white ones of the lady. She was stunned. 'A family of your own . . .'

April was far from stupid. Things had been moving beyond her lately . . . the way the boys treated her, the disapproval growing about her in the village. Once she had thought she could carry on being a child forever but now she knew it was impossible. And here was this woman, this posh lady, saying, 'when you have children . . . when you have a family of your own . . .' Barbara stood behind her, her warmth on April's back, holding her hands as softly as if they were birds. April

55

stared down at her plate as if a vision were opening up among the mashed potatoes. Then she straightened her shoulders and cut her sausage neatly in two. She looked up anxiously for approval.

'Wonderful! Wonderful! You see, Tony . . . she can do anything if she wants to try. Can't you, darling?'

April nodded. Yes, it was true, she could do anything. Tony considered that she looked like an ape doing tricks and he began to snigger but to his surprise his mother drove her sharp heel down with such violence onto his shoe that he screamed.

'Can't she, Tony?' smiled his mother sweetly. Tony nodded and blinked his watering eyes.

Her eyes on Barbara, April imitated the way she lifted the food to her mouth and chewed with small movements of her jaw. She even imitated the refined smile of appreciation on her face.

'Wonderful!' repeated Barbara. 'Wonderful!'

April was a clever mimic and by the end of the meal she was eating like a princess. When Barbara began to discuss the making of a gooseberry pie the girl tried to explain in her gruff, incoherent voice how to do it. Barbara frowned in concentration, but the girl glanced at Tony and fell silent. She was ashamed of her voice and remained dumb in the presence of all but her most trusted friends, of whom Barbara Piggot had already become one. But before she ran off she indicated by mime that she would be back to help with the pie that evening, and was overcome with delight when the wonderful lady leant over and kissed her cheek in gratitude.

When she had gone, Barbara rose and rubbed her hands together. She felt definitely better. She was getting on top of it already.

'Now, I suggest you make your contribution by doing the washing-up,' she began, but stopped when she saw her son's face. 'Oh dear. Are you still cross with me, darling?' Tony said nothing. She sat down by him and said, 'Is it all my fault?' When he still didn't reply she went on, 'Your father and I exchanged vows in church. It's rather silly really . . . promising to love someone. I wonder how many people really marry for love? Women . . . and children . . . have always depended on a man to provide for them.' She pressed her soft cheek to his and he wanted to melt to her. But he couldn't; not yet. Then she got up.

'I'm going upstairs to write a few letters and begin manoeuvres,' she told him. 'I don't know what you think about it but I'm sure you're grown up enough to understand right and wrong. Your father really ought to provide for us a bit better than this and I'm going to do my best to make sure that he does. Do try and help me, darling, won't you?'

Tony ignored the washing-up. He was feeling so crushed by claustrophobia that he overcame his shame at being seen emerging from the little hovel and went down to explore the river properly.

'Let the deaf girl do it,' he muttered to himself as he made his way down the road. He pretended to despise April, but deep down he had actually begun to admire her. It was the contrast with himself. He felt so stiff and trapped inside and April was so much alive. He thought of how she had silently explained to his mother that she would be back later to cook the pie. She had made herself as clear as glass without a word – her excited gestures, her intense, open face. She was so expressive. She made him feel as if he were made out of wood.

It was a warm day with a breeze, the blue skies scattered with small fluffy clouds. The river was beautiful today, its brown water sparkling in the sunlight and dashed into jewels by the wind. The tide was on its way in, the air smelt of the sea and decay. The seagulls were about, ducks, swans and geese were busy on the river. Along from the woodyard in a meadow of hollows and clumps of trees, the swallows, martins and swifts were congregating, some sweeping along the top of the grass for insects, others diving down to the edge of a small stream to scoop up a beakful of mud to build their nests.

Tony was immune to all this. He was sick with himself. He regretted that letter now. His Uncle Bob was trying to turn his mother into something like a prostitute. His father had deserted her. His father was a cad. At school, all boys had been proud of their fathers and defended them fiercely. He had once had a fight with a boy who called his father a bank clerk. He would do the same thing again, but now he knew that his father was a cad who had brought shame on them all. They had to live in a horrible place and his mother had to do shameful things because his father had let them down. If he could, Tony would have flown like a bird over the railways and snatched the letter back. But at the same time he could not help hoping . . .

Early that afternoon one of the railway porters came round with a big cardboard box – a gift from Uncle Bob. He sent crockery and cutlery, some pots and pans and other utensils, very good ones. The cutlery was silver and brand new. He had also sent a small hamper from a London store, containing tinned ham, expensive biscuits, relish, sauces, peaches in brandy and other delicacies.

'Get thee behind me, Satan,' murmured Barbara.

'We should throw them away,' said Tony unexpectedly.

'Yes, of course we should,' she replied. 'But we won't, will we?' she added with a smile. 'Although it's very sweet of you to think it. No. We shall sell the cutlery and anything else of value. And keep the hamper for special occasions.'

Tucked in the hamper was a large, white five-pound note which Barbara pressed to her bosom. 'Darling!' she cried. 'The money, not the sender,' she explained to Tony.

Tony put his nose in the air and said, 'We shouldn't accept it.'

'I'm so pleased you're taking such a high moral stance on it, darling,' she said, eyeing him with amusement and relief. 'But we have to live. We'll pay Bob back one day if it makes you feel any better. But right now, we'd better go shopping.'

When she suggested that he take over this errand, Tony agreed. He had dealt with shopkeepers before, although not for this sort of shopping. His mother had been through the cookery book and worked out recipes for the next few days. Together they compiled a list and ten minutes later he was setting off down to the village with the big wicker basket on his arm, feeling like a fool.

Tony successfully bought potatoes and cauliflower from the greengrocer. April had promised to bring the gooseberries from her garden, but his mother told him to buy apples in case she wasn't allowed. They could have the apples another day if their luck held and the gooseberries turned up. Then he went to Riley's, the grocer. In the window were piles of dusty tins and a cardboard cutout of a red-cheeked girl with short blonde hair and white smile, holding a basket of tinned peaches. Inside there were some advertisements pinned to the counter, for high chairs for sale, garden jobs needing doing, and so on. There was one in the grocer's own hand for a delivery boy five mornings a week. Tony paid Mr Riley the two pounds five and seven pence they owed and made his purchases. Riley called him 'sir' and he nearly fell over when Tony suddenly said, 'I'd like to enquire about the job advertised in the window. Would you mind telling me your terms of employment?'

By half past five, Barbara had taken out the bowls, the flour and fat necessary for the making of pies. She was actually rather excited at the idea and kept glancing at the illustration of steaming golden fruit pie that accompanied the recipe. She was horrified earlier when Tony came back and told her he had a morning delivery job. Her Tony, a delivery boy! But she put a brave face on it and pretended to be delighted, even though the money was a pittance that would do them no good at all. But the thought was there, and she was proud of him.

Time went by, but no April came. At a quarter past six, Barbara put on her hat and took a walk down the road to call for her.

She found April and her mother at their tea. Mrs Dean was delighted that April actually wanted to work and had, she explained, been intending to come round after tea to discuss 'terms'.

Barbara winced. Now she had to explain that she had no terms to offer. She explained the situation candidly, made much of her helplessness and of April's wonderful help. She impressed Mrs Dean by not being taken in by the usual village view that April was retarded in some way. But as she expected, Mrs Dean did not like the idea of April working for nothing.

But Barbara had the clincher up her sleeve. She got April, who was eating her tea in her slurpiest manner, to show off her new table skills. It was the first time since she was eight years old that her mother had seen her actually want to behave herself. Mrs Dean was delighted and charmed. If this lady could teach April to behave, it would be worth any amount of wages.

From then on, April spent several hours each day at the little house on the edge of the village. She usually came round in time to help cook breakfast and then, while Tony went to his job at the grocer's shop, she and Barbara did the housework and April collected her wages in the form of etiquette lessons.

Sometimes in the evening Mrs Dean came over to help with the evening meal and stayed to eat it, too. Afterwards the two women sat and talked about life with no husband, while Tony and April did school work that Barbara set them.

6

Mr Riley's grocery shop stood at the corner of the two
main streets in Cibblesham. It was a dark wooden shop
with high shelves neatly laid out with provisions, the
counter with the shiny brass scales and sacks stacked in
the corner full of meal and pulses, each with a dull silver
scoop resting inside. The shop had a strong sweet smell
that changed as you walked around it. In one place of
doormats and brooms and brushes it smelt of dusty
hemp. In another it smelt strongly of tarry soap; in
another was the sweet wheaty smell of loose biscuits.
The cheese and bacon were kept under glass bowls
behind the counter, and when they were uncovered an
intense smell of savoury salt, or the tang of the rich
yellow cheese made your mouth water.

Riley served the customers in a brown shop coat,
weighing and wrapping quickly and neatly while he chatted and peered keenly across at his customers. He smiled
a great deal while he was serving. His wife was a tall,
bony woman with enormous red hands who was always
working – lifting stock in and out of the back room,
taking deliveries which she carried like a man, or helping
in the shop.

'She's the brawn, I'm the brains,' Mr Riley told Tony,
and she smiled with her lips pressed together, a little
tiredly, Tony thought, and clapped her great big hands
with a loud crack. She took in laundry as well and spent
hours every day scrubbing away behind the shop up to
her elbows in soapy water.

'The wife's got a good heart but no charm,' explained
Mr Riley. That was true, she was a blunt woman who

always spoke her mind. But she got on well with the customers for all that.

Mr Riley regarded himself as being rather sophisticated and therefore good with the ladies and the more well-off customers. When he was serving a young woman he would become terribly courteous and gallant, opening doors and kissing their hands when his wife was out the back. He had his favourites with whom he was especially familiar. He sometimes tried to kiss them when they left; the young women leaned back and averted their faces. When the door closed and he was on his own with Tony, Riley narrowed his eyes and gossiped.

'She's a trollop,' he said. 'Had it away with half the village before John Forester got his hands on her.' He sighed and polished his spectacles. 'He won't keep her tied down for long,' he said, staring wistfully after her through the door.

He often made crude remarks about his female customers, watching Tony closely and nudging him as if they were old friends. 'What do you think of them?' he'd hiss with a nudge in the ribs, when a Mrs Thomson, a small woman with large breasts came into the shop. 'Bet she gives her old man a good time with them . . .' Tony was horrified with embarrassment. It had never occurred to him that a grown man might speak like that. It seemed certain that these women would know what was going on, but when Mrs Thomson turned round, Riley would become polite without a twitch. 'Madam?' he'd enquire, as if she were the Queen herself. He could turn his shop manner on and off at will.

Riley seemed to consider Tony a bit slow. 'All our local lads know what it's about by the time they're your age,' he told him. 'I did, anyhow . . .' In fact, like a lot of other boys at his boarding school Tony had played about a bit with some of the village girls. That was just walking in the dark and touching them up, but he found himself making much of these experiences to the grocer. He regretted it immediately. He only did it because he didn't want to seem a child. He wanted to share nothing with Riley that was private, although these experiences hadn't seemed particularly private before.

In the shop Tony wore a prickly woollen suit and a stiff white apron that he was supposed to keep spotlessly clean. His job was to tidy the shelves, sweep up, polish and clean, but especially to deliver groceries to the customers in the village and outlying houses. To do this he had a big black bike with a huge wickerwork basket on the front. He had to clean the bike every day before he went home so that it gleamed. Sometimes, while he was polishing, it reminded him of boarding school where he had to do similar jobs for Willis. At least he was being paid for it now, but it almost made him weep to think that for all this, he was getting just half a crown a week. Uncle Bob used to give him that just for carrying his bags out of the house to the car when he came to stay for the weekend.

Tony was fit from playing games at school, but the bike was built like a tank and it was really hard work pedalling up and down the roads, rattling over the cobbles and steering the laden handlebars round the potholes and kerbs. The customers were surprised, some disapproving, that a boy of his background should be delivering their groceries. Tony hated being pitied, but once they got used to it they became friendly and invited him in for tea or a bite to eat and tipped him rather better than they might another delivery boy. Riley nagged him not to accept invitations to step in, however, and Tony had to give up his little breaks. One or two of the customers complained about how Riley drove the boy, although they never had before when a little lad called Tommy Whites had pedalled panting up and down the lanes. Riley got round it by getting Tony to deliver to them last, so if he lingered, he ended up doing it in his own time.

The grocer was enormously proud of having a toff in to do his cleaning and delivering and he was by turns bullying or too chummy, as if he were the leader of a gang and Tony his favourite member. In the first week he often sent Tony on some errand to the back of the shop so that he could gossip about him to his customers. Tony could see them peering over at him, and his ears turned red. In this way, the news about him and his mother being destitute spread round the village like wild fire.

'Say hello to Mrs Hancock, Tony,' commanded Riley.

'Good afternoon, how are you?' said Tony formally, holding out his hand, and everyone roared with laughter at his accent and manners. After that he caught on and started saying, 'Morning, ma'am!' But the grocer was displeased.

'Say it like you used to,' he ordered.

'I don't like to,' complained Tony.

'While I'm paying you, you'll talk like I tell you,' said Riley with satisfaction. Actually Mr Riley was having a good week. His custom had increased with people coming in to see his novelty delivery boy. He was very proud of his business sense. But he didn't like Tony to talk too posh. Once, a customer from one of the outlying farms called by but when she spoke to Tony he couldn't make out a word she said. After four or five attempts, he exclaimed, 'But it's incomprehensible!'

The woman laughed, but Riley was most displeased when she left the shop. 'I don't want you using words like that in my shop,' he scolded. 'You'll put my customers off. We don't have words longer than "marmalade" in a grocer's shop!' And he laughed at his own joke.

Tony wasn't all that good at the job – not fast enough or clean enough, Riley told him. 'I'm only doing it as a favour to your mother,' he said. It pleased him to think he was doing a classy lady like Mrs Piggot a favour. On the third day he winked at Tony and slipped a pound of best bacon into his pocket. 'Not a word to Mrs Riley,' he added, glancing to the back of the shop, where his wife was pounding the laundry. 'She watches the stock like an eagle, the Missus.' He puffed himself up and watched his delivery boy stammering his thanks. 'She's a good woman, your mother. Tell her, Mr Riley will be happy to help out when he's able.' Riley liked to make out he was some kind of saviour to them, with his half a crown a week and his pound of bacon. He boasted about it to the customers. Tony had to appear grateful and he very quickly came to loathe the grocer.

Towards the end of the first week, April came in. Tony was dusting the displays in the shop window, but Riley called him out. 'Help keep an eye on her, she's light-fingered,' he whispered.

Tony smiled cautiously at her. He was more used to her now, he saw her at his house every day. April adored his mother, but Tony hadn't made friends. He was beginning to realise there was more to her than met the eye, but he was still uncomfortable. She grinned at him and chuckled at his apron and uncomfortable look.

'We haven't seen you in here for a while, lovey,'

bellowed Riley at her. He turned to Tony. 'She doesn't understand much, but she likes the attention,' he informed him. Tony glanced at April who looked back impishly. She was watching Riley's face. Tony was certain she knew exactly what he was saying but she didn't let on and neither did he. But April was less pleased with herself when the grocer started to gossip about her.

Riley smiled at her and went on. 'I feel sorry for her really. She was a sweet little thing when she was little, but when a girl like that grows up ...' April glanced anxiously at Tony. She looked sullen and turned away, but the grocer didn't link it with what he'd just said.

'Not surprising, the way she's turned out,' Riley continued, pulling a face and cutting cheese. Tony tried not to look interested, but he was. Riley knew everything. 'On her own. No discipline. Her mother's no better ... off every weekend with some chap. No man about the house. The girl just does what she likes.' He lowered his voice to a hiss as he always did with a juicy piece of gossip, although April was deaf.

'She's always mucking around by the river with the lads. Two, three of 'em at a time. She doesn't know any better. Oh yes.' He pursed his lips and nodded rapidly. 'Half the lads in the village have had her. Well, I don't blame them, but it's no good, they'll have to do something about it in the end. Everyone knows ... the vicar and everyone. She'll get a bun in the oven and they'll have to put her away where she can't do any harm. You can't have young girls running wild like that, you've got to think of the lads, what are they supposed to do? Oh yes ...' April was away at the other end of the shop. She glanced nervously round. Riley nodded, smiled and waved. Tony smiled vaguely. He believed it all.

'She's not so bad today but sometimes ... well, she doesn't leave much to the imagination. I've had an eyeful before now I can tell you. Here ... I'll show you what ...'

Riley glanced back to see if his wife was about. Then he shouted, 'Oy, April,' and stamped hard on the wooden floor. April jumped and looked around her; she could hear the noise but didn't know at first where it came from. Riley beckoned and she came forward. As she drew up, he pretended to have a query about the list and as he leaned across to her he knocked the pile of polished brass weights off the counter. They fell and banged on the wooden floor.

'Oh, silly me!' he exclaimed. April bent to pick them up, but he leaned over the counter and seized her shoulder to stop her. He pointed with his fingers at the list and at the same time spoke. 'Tony, you get round and pick 'em up and see if you can't get a look up her skirt,' he commanded. 'Ten to one she's not got any knickers on. Go on ... see what you can see ... before she starts picking 'em up herself.'

Tony was horrified. He stared at Riley but the man was clueless. April gave nothing away. She cocked her head to one side. Her eyebrows may have been very slightly raised. And she waited.

'Go on, go on, quick. What are you, a sissy? Go on ...' Riley nagged excitedly.

Tony hated Riley for his crudeness and his gossiping, and hated him now for behaving like a stupid boy. He was frozen with embarrassment but he didn't want to be a sissy. He should have said coldly, 'She understands every word you say,' but instead he found himself going round the counter and getting down on all fours at April's feet. April stood still and watched him. She stared at the back of his neck, which had gone red. Tony stared at the shiny wooden floor, at April's brown sandalled foot that had traces of mud between her neat small toes. He could smell her skin. Around her foot were the bright metal weights.

'Go on, go on,' nagged Riley. 'You won't see nothing staring at the floor. Look up . . . you'll get an eyeful, I'll bet. She don't care, she likes it.'

Tony wanted to turn his head to smile apologetically at April, but to do that he really would have to look up her skirt. He raised his head until he could see into the shadow above the hem of her skirt and looked suddenly away with a thrill of embarrassment, excitement and shock. He was in a complete daze.

'Here . . . I'll give you a hand!' exclaimed Riley, and he almost ran round the counter. But as he came round the corner, April quickly seized the hem of her skirt and sank down to her haunches, pulling her skirt tight about her feet and pressing her knees together. Her face was almost on a level with Tony's. She smiled right at him, her eyes bright, her lips moving in amusement. Tony smiled weakly back, relieved that she was smiling . . . and disappointed . . .

Riley had fallen to his knees at her feet, panting. April turned to look at him with that empty, bird-like expression she reserved for idiots. He began picking up the weights. 'Not quick enough,' he said accusingly at Tony. His little eyes twinkled angrily. 'You're not going to get anywhere like that,' he said. He got to his feet and went round the corner to finish the order.

Later when she had gone, the grocer added, 'She likes you I reckon. You could have her if you wanted. Dirty little beast, she is. But I don't know.' He sniffed and gazed at the door. 'I wouldn't fancy it meself,' he said, pulling an ugly face. 'Be like doing it with an animal ...'

Whenever he thought of the incident Tony broke into such a cold sweat his clothes stuck to his skin. But he couldn't get it out of his mind. When he got home that evening April smiled at him and he looked quickly away. She giggled, which he hated. He thought of her differently from now on. She had caught his eye against his will. He found himself watching her ... her face, her bare arms, her legs, the tops of her breasts under her collar or through the sleeves of her blouse. When they stood close together he was aware of her warmth and the scent of her skin and sweat. He got so conscious of it that she only had to approach him and he suffered a shock. When she saw him looking, April looked back and he turned red. Sometimes she smiled but he never smiled back. He thought she might be laughing at him.

Although she was a little anxious at the way he looked at her, April was charmed too because no one had ever looked at her like that before. She had been ogled often enough, but then she had felt victimised. Poor Tony was his own victim. At first she tried to smile at him, but he got embarrassed. So she moved about her tasks for Barbara and pretended not to notice. But she enjoyed the feel of his eyes on her. A year ago she might have played up and shown off, now she felt the need to cover herself up more. When she felt her blouse was opening too far, or her skirt riding up her leg, she tugged her clothes into place and glanced at him and smiled excitedly to herself.

7

During the week, Barbara borrowed Mrs Dean's bicycle and cycled to Redcliffe to sell the silver cutlery Uncle Bob had sent them. That got them another six pounds seven to add to the five-pound note. She spent some of the money on crockery and some cheap cutlery that tasted of tin, but there were still pounds left over. Her monthly allowance of ten pounds arrived on Wednesday in a plain envelope with no note. As far as her husband was concerned, they had been living off nothing at all since Saturday.

Before she took her trip into town, she and Tony went through their possessions to see what else might be sold. Tony had nothing but his school uniform, some spare clothes and some books. His mother had what she had travelled with when she returned to find her house closed, some ten suitcases of clothes and jewellery. She kept the best 'to make an impression when I have to,' she told Tony, and put the rest aside to be sold whenever they needed the money.

She also put an advertisement in the local paper advertising tuition in French, German and singing. Rather than waste time arranging this by post she charmed Riley into letting her use his phone number. Tony saw what she meant by making an impression. She dressed up in a posh frock, called him 'such a sweet man, and so charming' and took off her gloves to dust the flour off his brown work coat with her bare hands. Riley couldn't say yes quick enough, but Mrs Riley was not so pleased. Normally her husband only ever did his flirting when she was out of sight, but Barbara was merciless. Maybe the fact that his wife was watching as she flicked the flour off his chest and laid her hands on his arm made him agree all the more quickly. Tony could see Mrs Riley looking grimly out of the storeroom door. In her thick apron and workclothes, all dusty and sweating from cleaning, she looked like another species from Barbara altogether.

Tony hated it, too. Since she claimed to be so virtuous he didn't see what right she had to flirt with the likes of Riley for the sake of a few free phone calls. The grocer never made remarks about his mother but Tony could guess the sort of thing that was in his mind. He complained but his mother just laughed and told him it should be a warning to him not to be taken in himself by a pretty face.

Riley took the phone calls and ran with the messages personally. He called when he knew Tony was out delivering and always brought some little present – ham, a thick slice of cheese, a potted chrysanthemum. Barbara let him peck her cheek and told him not to tell.

Earning extra money for a few weeks was one thing but in the long term Barbara had no intention of working for her keep. Her husband owed her a living and she meant to get it. In that first week she posted over thirty letters. She was not ready yet to go to law. The whole thing might blow over. Elliot might find living with his mistress rather different from what he expected . . . and besides, what good would a divorce do her? She would get a settlement, no doubt, but it would not be the sort of household Barbara intended for herself. He supposed that a few weeks of poverty would soften her up, but he would find differently. There would be no such settlement.

72

A great many people liked and admired Barbara Piggot and some of them had very influential positions. She knew dukes, lords and earls, their sons and daughters, their friends and families. She had one good friend whose father was a director in her husband's bank. Reputation was everything to a man in her husband's position; the bank hated any scandal and Barbara was prepared to be very public if she had to be. To this friend and to others she wrote her letters and began to draw a web around her husband with which she intended to squeeze the sense back into him.

Barbara had no illusions about her situation. There were very few jobs for a woman of her class even if she wanted one. Women like herself were usually either married or had money of their own. Having Tony made it even more impossible. Even her dearest friends would not be keen on having a penniless woman and her teenage son as permanent house guests, and she had no expectation of being rescued. But she might be helped. She asked for nothing but told her best friends what had been done to her and asked for their advice.

On Friday morning the postman pushed ten letters through the door.

There were exclamations of anger and sympathy . . . and there was help. By the time the letters were all open their wealth had increased by sixty pounds, a small fortune. They laughed and laughed, because here they were in poverty with this great pile of money in front of them, the most money Tony had ever seen.

Tony's half-crown a week that he thought would help pay their way looked suddenly pathetic, even though Barbara assured him it was all the more valuable because it was steady money they could rely on. But for now the relief at having money to pay for their food and clothes was indescribable. Mother and son began to dance around the table and even fling the precious notes in the air, their paper treasure.

When things died down they read the letters greedily. Barbara put on her reading glasses and read out loud, but she tucked the letters out of sight when he tried to come behind to read, too.

'Why not?' he begged.

'Private,' she teased.

He was too curious so she put the letters away and talked instead about the money. They agreed to spin it out as long as they could. April and her mother were helping them, they had little jobs and now this pot of gold. They were out of the dark . . . for the time being.

'This will be like a little holiday for us,' smiled Barbara. She kissed her son's cheek, enclosing him for a moment in her sweet scent. 'When the winter comes, we'll be out of here,' she promised. They put the money in a pot in the cupboard and promised themselves to raid it only once a week.

Later when his mother was out, Tony crept into her room to find those letters. He would never have done this before, but now it had begun he had to know everything. He soon found what he was looking for.

In some ways it was unfair. No doubt his father had his own tale to tell. No doubt Barbara did not tell her friends everything. But when Tony had finished reading he had no doubt about the sort of man his father was.

Tony went to his room to weep . . . for shame for his father, for shame for himself. Now he thought his mother was magnificent, even though she sometimes let herself down as with her behaviour to Riley. He swore to himself she would always remain like this, as far above the likes of his father and Uncle Bob as the sun was above the clouds.

There was no mail for him that week or the week after. He was ashamed of himself and glad that he'd had no reply.

Cibblesham village was intrigued. The woman and her son who had come to live among them had obviously been badly treated by someone although no one knew the exact details, except Mrs Dean who kept it to herself. Mrs Piggot was a remarkable woman, they all agreed. Although obviously well-bred she did the housework with every evidence of pleasure, helped by the deaf idiot April, who doted on her. She refused to wear ordinary clothes for this work but had got hold of a man's boiler-suit which she dyed bright blue and wore with a tight red belt around her waist. She tied her hair up in a bright cotton headscarf and could be seen in this strange dress scrubbing her front step and even strolling down the High Street to shop.

Every now and then, for no apparent reason, she would take off her working clothes and put on one of her best frocks. April would dress up in the pretty skirts her mother got for her, Barbara helped her with her make-up and did her hair. Then she would put her big wicker basket on one arm, take the girl on the other and the two of them would go out for a stroll or shopping like a pair of fine ladies on an outing. Anyone who didn't know April would never guess that she played in the mud half naked, knew nothing and understood less. She looked for all the world like this expensive lady's favourite daughter.

Her son, too, was coping well. A lad like that, who could read Latin – everyone knew this, as he had translated the motto on a tin of chutney for one of the customers – and doubtless do all sorts of other educated things, serving in a common shop and delivering . . .! His manners were a delight to behold, but it wasn't right. The vicar was concerned that the common people might get funny ideas, being served by a member of what he called 'the governing classes'.

'The boy will give people funny ideas,' he told Barbara one Sunday after church. 'It's bad for morale.'

The Russian revolution and the death of the Tsar were only a few years old. People were beginning to see the Great War that had ended only seven years ago not as a patriotic sacrifice, but a mass slaughter of ordinary people by those in charge. The vicar didn't want people to get any funny ideas about the ordering of society.

'Oh, dear!' observed Barbara, and did nothing whatever about it.

All Cibblesham gossiped. So far, the gossip was friendly – about where they came from, what had happened to them, where they were going, how they were coping. Everyone was interested. But there was one person whose life was completely changed by the new arrivals.

April hadn't been born deaf. She could hear well enough up to the age of five, when she had her accident.

Typically, she should have been in school when it happened. Her mother left her that morning in the playground and went on her way. When April didn't turn up in the classroom the teacher assumed she was off that day, until an hour into lessons when one of the children mentioned having seen her in the playground earlier. A search was begun; it did not last long.

They found April lying on the flags on the other side

of the wall that lined one edge of the playground. It was a high wall, six feet tall with high black railings on top. April had wanted to climb it ever since she started school and had hidden behind the dustbins to get a chance at it while the others were in assembly and no one was watching. As she carried her inside, her teacher, Mrs Hall, saw the blood running from both ears and feared the worst.

From that day the world of sound died for April to a kind of sea of boomings and mutterings that came from all around her. She knew how to talk, of course, but she learned only a few more words than those she knew on that day when she was five years old. Her speaking deteriorated as she made her voice sound more and more like the voices she heard when people yelled at her. And her behaviour got worse.

April was furious. She felt people were talking about her all the time, even to her face. As the full impact of her disability sank in she became more and more frustrated and aggressive, and she began to withdraw into herself rather than torment herself with a world she could no longer understand. When her father died a year after the accident, things got even worse. It had always been her father who imposed the discipline in the house. Her mother, suddenly on her own fighting to keep her home together, had no time to give April the attention that she needed. She became impossible to control and people began to believe that the fall had damaged her mind as well.

Nothing could be further from the truth. April might howl and run away or hit you in the stomach if you annoyed her, but she knew everything that was going on around her. She very quickly learned to lip read but most people took the intense stare with which she watched their faces as another sign of mental disturbance. For them, April was deaf and dumb, with the emphasis on the dumb. April did not disillusion them. In fact, she liked it. They looked down on her; this enabled her to look down on them.

She attended the local school for a while, but she was too disruptive. Her mother had to work and there was nothing for it but for the little girl to be farmed out to friends and helpers. As the years went by April became more and more cut off from the village life by her deafness, by her refusal to communicate, by the lack of care. By the time she was twelve she ran wild, in and out of people's houses, pinching food from the shops and spending as much time as she could away from the village, on the river banks on her own. At first people tolerated this well enough; she was a sort of mascot, the village idiot. But the time came for her to grow up and April could not seem to do it. It seemed that her injury had left her forever a child, leaving her body to grow up without her.

The mood changed. The village became ashamed and angry.

April was well aware of this. As she became aware she became more and more frightened at the threats to her freedom and safety . . . from the boys who caught her on her own, from the doctor who wanted her certified, from the vicar who wanted her out of the way in case she corrupted the young men. It seemed to everyone, even her mother and her friends, that she was doing everything she could to resist change but in fact she was desperate to find a way into the grown-up world. But there was no school, no social life, no training, nothing. It was clear – the village had made it clear – that she could never become like one of them. This was believed so much and so widely that April had come to believe it herself. The way out simply did not exist.

It was just then that Barbara and Tony Piggot turned up.

They needed her. They were clever and people looked up to them, but they were helpless just like her and they needed her. For the first time in her life, April found in Barbara a grown-up person she wanted to be like. She tried to look like her, walk like her, do everything like her, as if she could take her life on by copying her. When her mother, delighted by her girl's new sense, bought her clothes, April always wanted to wear the same colours and styles as her new friend. When Barbara gave her one of her scarves, April was as thrilled as if she had been given jewels. She hung the creamy coloured woollen scarf, with its brown tassels, on her wall and only ever wore it for best when she was with Barbara herself. She took to wearing her bra and so long as she was in the village did her best to look like a proper young lady. But although times were changing, class rules were still rigid. Poor April had as much chance of turning into a lady as she had of growing wings and flying to the moon.

And there was Tony. He was so shy. She couldn't believe that someone like him could be shy of someone like her. He was ashamed but so curious about her and she loved those hot little glances he cast. When she was about the house she wore the new clothes her mother had bought her and she watched secretly for the flicker in his eyes when she stretched up to hang washing on the rack or leaned across the table to reach something on the other side. She often thought about Jenny and her boyfriend. She hated Tad but she was jealous of Jenny because it had always seemed impossible to her that any boy could be interested in her, the dummy, the idiot, the deaf girl. She was all right to hold down and poke and pinch, but . . .

'Kiss her, go on,' said Tad to Joe once, on one of those terrible attacks the summer before. April lay with her dress rucked up around about her neck and couldn't move an inch, with the weight of two boys on her arms and legs.

'Kiss your girlfriend, Joe,' sneered Tad.

And Joe pulled a face and spat, a little blob of shiny disgust that landed on her face and trickled down, getting cold, into the rushes underneath.

Of all the things they had done to her, rude and cruel, that was the worst somehow, and April recalled the taunt, 'kiss her', so many times it seemed impossible that anyone ever would.

The greatest gift Barbara and Tony Piggot brought to April was the freedom from fear. She spent the weekends at the Piggots' house for as long as she could, cleaning the place from top to bottom. At night she had to go home, of course, but she felt that somehow, her new friends were protecting her even when they weren't there. The incident at her house was not repeated. Tad had even spoken quite seriously to her when she went to visit Jenny and found him there. The boy was only doing this to please his girl; secretly he shared the view that April was an idiot. On the street, too, the boys treated her differently. They looked at her and laughed, which wasn't good but not so bad as the jeering and ogling she used to have to put up with.

Her friends, Mr and Mrs Giles, old Mrs Craddock and Jenny, were all delighted.

'There, you see,' Jenny told her. 'You can be so pretty

if you want to be.' But she added sadly, 'What a shame you'll never be able to marry and have a proper family . . .'

In the mornings April helped Barbara but the afternoons were for her old life, which was still for her the only true one. She put on her old shirt and frock, although she left the bra on all the time now, and ran off down the river bank – to boat, to catch song birds, to fish or search for snakes or eels in the reeds. And at least once a week, April did her utmost to catch a mate for Silas the swan.

The swans knew April well. As soon as they saw her coming they began to glide away and if she got too close they ran across the water and took to the sky. She had to creep up close and jump but at this time of year they were nesting and usually found in pairs. If you got hold of one, the other would attack, and they were powerful birds. They could rip the flesh with their bills and strike with their long, muscly necks. After several nasty fights, April had come to be scared of the swans. She wanted a net, really, but had no money. Several times she had tried to steal one from one of the fishing boats that occasionally moored in Cibblesham, but had so far failed.

On Wednesday afternoon April devised a new plan. She borrowed four good thick blankets off her mother, without her mother knowing, and stitched them roughly together to make one huge spread. She then hid herself up in a tree, an old willow overhanging a bed of mud that became exposed at half tide. A young female swan, not yet old enough to mate, often used this patch of mud to sit on and preen herself. She could be seen standing on one black leg watching the water go by almost every day.

April concealed herself in the tree as the water drained out of the estuary towards the sea. Soon the rounded back of the mud bank rose to view. April had been stuck up her tree for over an hour and she was getting cramp when the swan appeared, flying downstream from her feeding grounds in the fresh water further up river. She flew straight for the mud bank and crashed into the water, splaying her legs and wings clumsily. Then she ruffled her feathers and began to glide serenely towards the hump of mud. April held her breath. The swan climbed up out of the water, wagging her tail like a dog. April waited a little longer, until the bird settled down directly beneath her hiding place, seven feet up in the branches of the willow.

April dropped like a stone, the blanket spread on her hands and feet. She landed just to one side of the bird with a great slap onto the mud and jumped sideways to cover her catch. With a violent explosion of wings, the swan leapt for the sky directly into the falling blanket.

It was a violent struggle and April knew she had lost as soon as the bird got its neck out from the side of the blanket. She was terrified of being pecked and cringed back as it opened its bill wide and pecked and hissed. The gap opened; the swan caught her ear and ripped it with a jerk of its powerful neck. April screamed and backed away: the swan fled. It leapt off the mud bank flapping and hissing, its bum waggling as it paddled desperately on the water. In its panic, the bird fell neck first over another little mud bar and crashed into the water again. A second later, filthy with mud, it emerged once more running across the water. It finally took off over twenty feet away and began flapping as fast as it could along the river.

Bleeding freely, April crawled out of the mud pulling her sodden, muddy blankets after her. Her ear stung viciously. Holding her head and shaking the water and blood off her face, she got up onto the grass in time to see her swan fly up river, low to the water in a straight line next to the bank. And walking along that same bank, only seconds away from the swan, was Tony Piggot. In seconds they would pass within feet of each other.

Seizing her blanket and forgetting that she did not want to use her voice with him around, April ran at him shouting at the top of her lungs, 'The swan! Get it . . . Get the swan!'

So long as you regarded it as a kind of camping holiday it wasn't so bad. Then even that tiny little house was all right. They were roughing it for the summer, that's all. The worst bit was working for Riley but the rest of it was okay, really okay. All that money coming through the letter box had made him feel a lot better. He didn't miss his school. He certainly didn't miss his father. Here there was the river and the warm weather coming and his mother. His mother made him happy. Before she had been affectionate and charming but distant. Now she told him everything, nearly . . . treated him as her equal and once he got over the shock, he felt close to her for the first time in his life. She was dealing with everything. She would deal with his father. He was proud of the way people looked up to her even though his father had tried to humiliate her.

Today, on a sunny afternoon in the beginning of June, Tony walked along the bank with a towel with a pair of torn trousers wrapped in it under his arm. He was looking for a place to go swimming. A few days ago at this time he had dipped in off the jetty. There was a mist on the water that day, and he had left the sun behind when he jumped in. It was secretive, swimming under the layer of mist. He felt like a spy, stealthy and predatory, but it was cold, too, and he hadn't stayed in for long. Today the sky and water were clear and bright, but Tony wasn't yet used to the changing times of the tides. Now the mud was back, and he was walking by the river looking for a spot where he could reach the water without getting filthy getting in and out. There was no such place.

He was about half a mile out of the village when there was some sort of an explosion on the mud ahead of him. A blanket fell out of a tree and began screaming. The blanket thrashed violently about in the mud and suddenly a swan shot out from under it and came hurtling towards him. A second later April emerged, bleeding down the side of her head and covered in mud and slime. She was trailing the giant blanket after her, but when she spotted him she got violently excited and came running at him, yelling at him in a furious, chaotic voice. He thought he could make out the word 'Wan!' over and over.

The swan was flying determinedly, rising slowly, some four feet above the ooze, level with the bank. It had seen him but even though he would be able to reach out an arm and touch its wing as it flew past, it did not change its course. Perhaps it felt safe because the water was so far below it. What had it to fear? It was in the air, flying fast. The boy meant nothing. Further along the bank, April made a scooping motion with her blanket and Tony realised she wanted him to catch the swan in his arms.

84

Sometimes on the rugby field at school, as a player three times his size went hurtling towards him, Tony's mind would go through a series of rapid calculations. He'd work out all the details: the speed he had to jump, when to jump, where to jump, his opponent's likely course of action. The only thing he would leave out would be the fact that the player was built like a rhinoceros and would probably flatten him. And his body, without him even wanting it, would jump into a tackle. Now, to his amazement, his mind did exactly the same thing. The swan would be about three feet away, its pinions could brush his face. He would have to jump when the wing was in a downward flap. The mud was six feet below them. He would catch it around the neck, lie on its back and glide down to the ground. And then he dropped his towel and jumped.

As he jumped he realised how idiotic that last thought was. To ride a swan! Then Tony and the swan collided with a heavy thud.

It knocked the breath out of him and he heard the swan gasp, too. He wrapped his arms round the serpent neck, hid his head and down they went, flailing arms and wings into the sticky estuary mud. A voice from the past – someone at school – said in his ear, 'A swan can break a man's arm with a single blow of its wing' and Tony climbed on top of it and tried to get the wings wrapped to its sides like a chicken, but these were dragon's wings and as soon as he got one tucked in the other flared up. Meanwhile the long neck struck at him. Tony buried his head in the crisp white feathers and the swan tore at his scalp. It hurt like hell but he didn't care because he had actually snatched this great white beast out of the air like a miracle. Then came a huge wet slap as April dived in with him. The gigantic blanket thing hung for a second in the air above him and everything turned black.

By the time he unwrapped himself, April had covered the swan in soggy blanket and was dragging it out. He scrambled to help her and together they pulled the bird, flapping slowly like a dying monster, out of the mud and onto the bank.

'It was like a rugby tackle . . . it was flying . . .' babbled Tony excitedly. April was grinning at him as she tied a huge wet knot in the blankets. 'It weighed a ton . . . they can break your arm but it couldn't get me, I was too close . . .'

April suddenly finished her knot and flung herself at Tony. She came so hard she knocked him down. Tony stared at her in astonishment from the ground. April glared back at him, because that wasn't what she had meant to do, not at all. Then she grinned, held her arms above her head and whooped joyfully. Tony was too excited to mind. He grinned and scrambled up. Such a thing to have done!

'Did you see me get it? In the air?' he gasped. He paused, thinking she couldn't understand. In fact he was talking so fast she couldn't get a word of it but April nodded excitedly. She was strung between her own excitement and the enormous frustration that was building up inside her because she had no way of telling him how wonderful he was.

'It was flying!' exclaimed Tony again. He began to tell her . . . how he had jumped, how he had fought, how the swan had tried to fly beneath him. He began to dance with excitement around the bird, whose wings still flapped, muddy and heavy now, a million miles from the open air. April glared at him, stared so intently at his face that Tony was beginning to feel uncomfortable.

Suddenly April jumped forward and seized him. She grabbed his head like a wrestler and twisted it so that he was directly staring into her own face. She gripped his head like a vice and stared ferociously at him, determined to speak clearly for once in her life and tell him how long she had wanted a mate for Silas, how hard she had tried and above all, how much she loved and adored him for getting one for her. It hurt. Tony let her force his head down and winced. April stared at him as if he were her deadliest enemy. She was only trying to get him to concentrate, to listen to her. She wanted to bellow her words at the top of her lungs to try and get him to understand but she knew from experience that all she would do was hurt him.

April quivered with frustration; her fingers dug painfully into his skin. Then he felt her sigh. Her anger seemed to melt suddenly inside her and she leant against him. Tony was still bending close to her face, waiting. Without knowing why, only because he was waiting and she had nothing else to do, she leaned up to him, turned his head and breathed her warm breath right into his ear.

Tony looked at her in astonishment out of the corner of his eye. Instinctively he turned and took her in his arms and they held one another very softly. They stood for a minute like this. April sighed and leant her head against him. They were pressed together full length and he could feel her breasts against him. A creeping embarrassment came over them both as they realised what they were doing.

Tony tensed and pushed her away. They stared at each

87

other. On the grass beside them the swan gave one last great flap and then lay still, exhausted, waiting.

'You've got two swans now!' Tony told her. April smiled shyly. She raised her hands in the air and shook them. 'It was flying!' yelled Tony. The two children, wild with excitement, began to dance around the captive bird, whooping and yelling at the top of their voices.

They carried the swan home between them wrapped up in the blanket. Then they had to get her into the kennel and tied up. Both the new swan and Silas hissed like kettles the whole time, but when it was all over Silas positioned himself outside the entrance and guarded his new mate, striking out even at April if she went near. The new swan, whom April christened Sissy, stayed in the dark and wouldn't let anyone near, not even Silas.

When he finally got home, Tony's mother was horrified to see him covered in blood and the stinking river mud. She was furious, but it was worth it. The next day April turned up first thing in the morning and dragged him round to see the new swan. Silas still stood proudly on guard outside the kennel and hissed ferociously. Sissy remained hidden inside, but her long neck would come snaking out for crusts of bread, which Silas greedily tried to eat before her.

April left early that evening, leaving Barbara to struggle alone with the dinner. The next day she came with a present for Tony, a linnet in a little wicker cage. It wasn't a colourful bird, with an untidy little red cap on its head. The cage was wonderful. April explained with gestures that she had woven it herself out of reeds. Tony hung the bird by his bed. The following morning it woke him with a sudden, glorious burst of song, sounding incredibly loud in his little room. He was enchanted

88

to have this hedgerow song inside with him but he had to beg a scrap of thick cloth from Mrs Dean to cover the bird, otherwise it woke him up at four o'clock every morning.

8

That weekend Mrs Piggot had a trip to make – to see an old friend, she told Tony. But first she had to wait at home for another visitor. Uncle Bob was coming.

Tony couldn't wait to be free of his uncle, who had tried to turn his mother into something very little better in his eyes than a prostitute. He went cold when he thought how he had cavorted in front of the car, shouting, 'Thank you, sir, thank you!' over and over. How gutless the man was for pretending he was doing him a favour!

'Tell him to . . . stuff himself,' he demanded.

Mrs Piggot laughed at her fierce son. 'Shall I?'

'He's a beast. I'll back you up,' said Tony, although he was scared of his uncle.

'Then we will,' she promised. 'It'll be something to look forward to. Only, not yet.'

'Why?'

'We aren't quite ready to be independent yet, I'm afraid. He is helping us out.'

Tony was enraged. It was immoral! 'But it's not a question of money!' he insisted angrily.

'Isn't it, darling?' Mrs Piggot rubbed her lip with the tip of a finger and looked at him.

'No, of course not. Taking money off him . . . it's the same as . . .' Tony blushed, furiously. '. . . as doing what he wanted. As being his mistress!' he said hotly.

Tony's mother herself blushed. What was he accusing her of? And was that a way for a son to speak to his mother? For a second she was full of rage. But she had started this line of talk. She bit back her anger and exclaimed, 'Scarcely the same, Tony!'

'What's the difference?' he demanded.

Mrs Piggot pursed her lips irritably. 'Well, apart from the obvious difference that I'm not sleeping with him,' she said brutally, and paused to watch him blush and turn away, 'apart from that – which does count for a little something, I think, darling – in this situation he is getting nothing from us and we are getting something from him. In other words, I'm in control.'

Tony wouldn't see it like that. Morals were morals, it didn't matter who was in control. He wanted his mother to be above everyone. But his mother was reluctant to give up the chance of more money from Bob until she had to.

Tony didn't want to see his uncle. He couldn't bear to pretend to be civil and he couldn't bear watching his mother pretending. He thought how she would say to him, no, she had not yet made up her mind . . .

'You're just stringing him along,' he shouted and ran out of the house. His mother ran a couple of steps to the door, but didn't call out as he ran down the road towards the railway bridge and the river.

'I shouldn't have told him,' she thought. He really was too young to understand these things.

When he had cooled down, Tony went to see April but she wasn't in. Of course she would be at his house. Tony waited until Uncle Bob's car had gone, and again until his mother left on the train before he went to look for her there.

Today April had promised to show him the river. She had made them sandwiches and a flask of milk, and they at once walked down to the boat moored by the jetty.

As April pushed out on to the water, the sounds of the land seemed suddenly muted. April rowed strongly downstream, gliding with the water's flow into another world.

It was so different on the water. Everything Tony thought he was familiar with now seemed new. Things that had been distant from the bank – the ripples on the water, the reeds, the half sunken branches, the hulks of old timbers stuck in the mud – all seemed to come to life as they approached them across the water. The land now was distant. This was the hidden world of the river.

April had never taken anyone here before. People were the village, the shops, the world of sound and chatter. This was her world. She showed him where the herons nested, where to catch flounder and plaice. They banked among the reeds and hunted for birds' nests suspended among the rushes. They drifted in the water, rowed across the water to see things close up – a tree, an island, a shape in the water – and then floated away again.

When they got hungry they climbed out and sat on the bank to eat their picnic. They sat a little apart and ate in silence. April was concentrating hard on eating nicely; it was hard not to make noises she couldn't hear. Tony had to touch her shoulder when he wanted to speak.

'I like it here,' he repeated. April frowned. 'I love it here,' he said loudly. April grinned and waved her arms all around to try and tell him that there was more, that it was endless, that it was all hers and that she wanted to show him everything.

On the way back they saw Tad and his friends sitting by the bank. The boys waved. Tony waved back. He felt it would be nice to have some other friends but not these big lads. Suddenly, he felt silly sitting next to the deaf mute. April rowed faster and wouldn't look.

When they got back to Tony's he found a note from his mother on the table that he had missed before. 'Back at 6.' He made a face and threw it on the fire. April went to the pantry and began looking for some food to cook. Mrs Piggot hadn't asked her, but April wouldn't have dreamt of letting her come home to no meal. Besides, there was Tony.

Tony watched her as she took the potatoes and began peeling them at the sink. He began to set the table.

Now that he had decided that the whole thing was a holiday, Tony didn't mind doing these menial tasks. He could describe it later to his friends as an adventure. 'We had to cook our own food,' he would tell them proudly. 'We had a deaf girl to help us and we taught her how to behave like normal.' After he had set the table, April got him to carry on peeling the potatoes while she set about chopping onions. There was minced meat in the pantry. April was going to make a shepherd's pie.

They worked in silence. Tony was learning to enjoy her wordless company. They did things together easily. If April wanted help, she waved or gestured at him to attract attention. She almost never used her voice and when she did, Tony looked at her in alarm. That put her off even more, of course, but it was not that he was disturbed by it any more. He'd come to forget almost that she had a voice and thought of her as so much a normal person that her groaning voice seemed to come from someone else.

April was a secret, his secret. The sort of person she was, the sort of things she understood were hidden to everyone except him. There were times when he felt this so strongly between them that he wanted to press his face close and whisper his own secrets in her ear. But what would be the point?

Barbara had eaten a late tea out and wasn't at all hungry, but she feigned delight that there was a hot shepherd's pie on the table. She pretended to be too excited to eat it.

'I've had a most successful day, a most successful day,' she announced, pulling off her gloves and sitting down at the table. April stared at her in awe. Mrs Piggot had dressed up in her best for this trip. She looked like a queen; she was a queen, in April's eyes.

Tony looked at her sideways. He wanted to know what had happened but he refused to ask her questions.

Barbara tasted her food and exclaimed that it was excellent. But she couldn't keep her news in any longer and suddenly put down her knife and fork and asked Tony, 'What do you say to a new house, darling? Shall we move?'

'Really? Really?' Tony forgot to be disapproving. April, not understanding because they were talking so fast, smiled nervously at their excitement. Tony began to ask questions suddenly. Will it be a big house? Will we have servants again? Will I start school . . . and so on. His mother smiled and kissed him.

'But nothing like that,' she said. 'We aren't out of the pit yet. But I have found someone willing to rent us a house for the summer. A friend. Nothing grand. He's not rich. Something small but pretty. We'll have to start looking first thing Monday morning.'

Tony looked at her crookedly. He was discovering he didn't quite trust his mother. 'Who is it?' he asked.

Barbara bit her lip and raised her eyebrows. 'Oh dear,

have I been bad? Do you want me to have a chaperone, darling?' She giggled. It really was too funny, the son worrying about his mother's morals! 'He's an old friend of whom I'm very fond, and of whom I used to be much fonder. I haven't seen him for years. He used to take me out. An old boyfriend and a kind, decent man. Is that all right, darling? Or would you like him to make an appointment to tell you his prospects?'

Barbara laughed. Tony began to smile . . . at her merriment, at himself. But he often remembered what she had said about mistresses . . . that one was supposed to love or like the man. He wondered what she would have said to Uncle Bob's offer if she had liked him.

He wondered how much she still liked this sudden new friend.

They found the new house on Monday, negotiated on Tuesday, moved in on Wednesday. It was on the main street, a small cottage with two bedrooms, a nice parlour to sit in, a small dining room and a kitchen. At the back was a garden with a child's swing and flowers growing through the weedy borders. It was fully furnished, a summer let that they had to give up by the winter, which pleased Tony and his mother better than a permanent home. Tony was already thinking of it as their 'holiday cottage'.

All they had were a few suitcases but Mrs Piggot quickly organised a team of helpers – April, of course, and her mother but also her friend Jenny and some of their new neighbours.

On Tuesday afternoon Barbara told April that she was going to show her what good manners and charm could do for you, if properly used. She dressed herself up, powdered her face and tied her hair up on top of

95

her head as if she was going to the theatre. She did the same with April and they walked out together to visit Mr Riley. In the shop, Barbara stepped among the barrels of dried peas and oats like a magnificent, elegant bird. April walked behind her, imitating her and coming out something like a small pheasant following a peacock. Mr Riley was terrified and Barbara gave a lovely demonstration to her pupil of how to wrap people around your little finger. In ten minutes she convinced the grocer to give her a lift in his van during the moving, and to let her have ten pounds' worth of goods on credit with the only condition 'that Mrs Riley never finds out'.

Tony was getting desperately curious about the man who was paying for all this but Barbara refused to tell him anything, past or present. It was so strange to imagine that his mother had another life apart from his father and himself, that there had been . . . that there were . . . other men who wanted her. Was she leading him on, as she was Uncle Bob? Or could such a gift be merely kindness, as she claimed?

Tony so badly wanted there to be someone really nice. 'If she likes him, who knows . . .' he thought. He accused her of having secrets. 'A lady never tells anyone anything – even if there's nothing to tell,' she teased. 'Aren't I allowed to have secrets from you?' she added. Which was a point. But she did promise that once they had moved in her friend would come to visit and Tony would see for himself.

On Wednesday at lunchtime the van turned up with Riley seated proudly in the front. Already the helpers had loaded everything into boxes and put them by the kerb ready to go. Tad turned up to be with his Jenny, which disturbed April. But the boys always behaved as if

96

nothing had ever happened. April had never told anyone about her ordeals, not even Mrs Piggot or her mother, and she was beginning to think of it all as a bad dream.

The helpers piled the boxes into the van. Barbara, magnificent in her boiler-suit with a tight belt around her waist and her hair in a silk scarf, climbed in beside Riley. Riley honked the horn and chugged slowly off with the others following behind. During the unloading Riley was bossy and officious, directing everyone and getting in the way and making grand promises about how he was going to help the family. He smiled under his moustache when Barbara approached him at the end to thank him. He presented her with a huge bunch of gladioli from his own garden and to Tony's everlasting disgust, got a kiss on his cheek for his efforts which made him blush with pleasure.

Barbara brought out a small table and chairs and everyone sat on the edge of the High Street and drank tea made by April and ate scones made by Helen Dean. People passing by stopped to chat and accept a scone. Riley went to the baker's and bought a cake when the scones ran out and was getting very lively indeed when Mrs Riley turned up. It was long past time to open the shop. Barbara apologised fully, but the grocer's wife was not impressed by any amount of charm, and it was a cowed Riley who was led off home by his wife.

Riley was a blot on the proceedings but Tony was wildly happy that day. The summer that had seemed so disastrous was turning out to be a festival. His mother was pulling it off . . . his mother could do anything. Once you realised that, everything was delightful. They had a place in the world that got better every day. Everyone liked them, everyone wanted to help. The last thing he wanted at that moment was to go back to his dull, hard, grey school life.

In the afternoon his mother went out to visit and Tony and April were left alone in the house. They wandered about the rooms, looking in the drawers, sitting in the chairs. Tony didn't mind her doing this with him; it was like looking through somebody else's house. He was in high spirits. April kept glancing anxiously at him but he didn't notice. In the sitting room he was looking at the coal scuttle, which had a ship embossed on its copper sides, when April came in beside him and took his hand. She led him through into the kitchen and paused. Tony waited. She was smiling shyly at him and he suddenly realised she wasn't taking him anywhere, she had nothing to show him.

The holding of hands suddenly meant something. It had never occurred to Tony that she wanted this, or that their friendship was like this, even though he was so conscious of her. April glanced at him and smiled anxiously, shyly. She wanted him to smile back but he couldn't. They began to walk together round the table, still holding hands awkwardly. They wandered into the dining room and then the sitting room. Tony was scared, he was struck dumb but April wanted to be closer still.

In the sitting room he bent close to her and said, 'Why can't you talk?'

Of course she didn't understand, he had no idea why he did it. It was because he wanted to be close to her. He was scared she would be offended but she smiled with pleasure. She had felt his warm breath on her ear, just as she had breathed on him when they had caught the swan. She smiled excitedly and leaned up and breathed back in his ear, warm and close.

Tony wanted to smile back but his face had frozen. She was terrified he wanted to get rid of her; he didn't know what to do next. Each was scared they were reading this all wrong. They stood front to front, touching, holding hands, excited, embarrassed.

April leaned up again and tipped her face up close to his.

He was worried she'd taste bad because there was something wrong with her. But she tasted as she smelled – a faint, dusky liquorice. When they had kissed Tony held her tightly, she leaned her head against him and they both heaved a sigh of relief. One spell was broken, another one had begun.

9

The new house was perfect, right in the village in the middle of everything. Every morning Tony was woken up by the smell of new bread from the bakery, three doors down. He could lean out of the window and talk to people as they walked, or shopped, and yet he could run down the road and be away by the river in three minutes. Barbara had rescued them into a new life that was getting better and better. There was only one thing that worried Tony now: who it was she had found to pay for this and what he wanted in return. On Sunday he had the chance to find out; Barbara had invited her friend to visit.

Barbara played the visit down. He was just dropping by. He'd probably take them out to a café for a cup of tea and a cake but it was nothing really, no special occasion. An informal visit by an old friend. But on Sunday morning, even though they had spent most of Wednesday and half of Thursday cleaning the house after moving in, Barbara decided suddenly after breakfast that it had to be done all over again. She dressed Tony and April in overalls and set them polishing, beating, scrubbing and shining as if the visitor had turned into royalty overnight. Barbara began absently dusting the china, but soon disappeared into her bedroom. She stayed there the whole morning, issuing instructions but refusing to come out.

The house was spotless and gleaming by eleven but it was another hour before Barbara appeared, transformed. She was dressed all in white – white skirt, white top, white blouse, white shoes and a droopy white hat that shaded her face with its snowy rim. She was spotless. The clothes she had worn to impress Riley and the villagers looked like gaudy rags. Tony thought he had never seen anything brighter, cleaner or more beautiful. Even her skin shone like rosy mother-of-pearl.

'How do I look, will I do?' she murmured, spinning round to show herself off. 'Not too formal . . .?' Then she caught a glimpse of the clock. 'Heavens, look! He'll be here in ten minutes . . .'

There was a loud groan of distress next to Tony. It was April. She was staring down at her own overalled body in disappointment and distress.

Barbara's hand flew to her mouth. 'Oh! I forgot utterly. He wants to see April too . . . quick!' She snatched the girl's hand and dragged her upstairs. 'Tony, get ready AT ONCE!' she snapped, as if the lateness was all his fault.

Tony was ready in ten minutes, but it took half an hour before Barbara had prepared April. She appeared in a fashionable blue gown to match her eyes and with hair coiled behind her neck. The gown was one of Barbara's own and it was a little too large. Tony felt shy of her. She kept glancing anxiously at him to see if he approved but he was too tongue-tied and confused by her sudden change from skivvy to beauty to open his mouth. Was it really April under there? She looked so different, so beautiful, he couldn't believe it was the same person.

Now they all began to wait for the arrival, all pretending to be lounging about doing something else. Used to the people at school or his parents' friends, Tony expected a car to pull up outside their house, and he stared at the man coming round the corner on a bicycle without ever dreaming who it was. Only when he dismounted and walked towards him with his hand out . . . 'Tony, is it?' did he realise who it was.

Their benefactor didn't look the part. He wore a cloth cap and his trousers were clipped to his legs. His legs were splashed with mud but he didn't seem bothered about it. Tony was incensed. When his mother came out to greet the man he looked like a farmyard chick next to a swan. The man eyed her suspiciously. 'You don't look much like cakes and tea,' he scolded. He looked at Tony and grimaced. 'Is there a Ritz in Cibblesham I can take her to?' he asked. Tony felt better then, but he stared angrily at his mother for over-dressing and showing them up.

The man introduced as David Price parked his bicycle in the porch and they all set off to a café further down the road. His cuffs were fraying, he had patches on his jacket and yet he seemed perfectly at ease with Tony's mother in all her glory. He chatted away, pointing out the sea birds . . . cormorants . . . sitting on the house tops, complimenting April on her dress and looks. April swanned along behind Barbara, keeping her eyes firmly fixed on the older woman as she tried to copy her elegant walk along the pavement.

Tony was unsure. Was the man poor, since he had frayed cuffs and an old suit? But he began talking about his work. He owned two bicycle shops and was thinking of opening a third. He worked in them himself, building racing machines for sportsmen! Not poor then, but not rich either. It all seemed eccentric and enterprising. Barbara floated, beautiful, by his side like something from another world. He had his hands in his pockets. He was kicking at stones and watching them rattle down the road.

Tony kicked at a stone himself; his mother frowned disapprovingly, but David winked and came up to talk ... about bicycles and boating and other stuff. He promised to bring a bicycle over for Tony to ride and one for April, too, if she wanted it. Tony could teach her, smiled the man. Tony nodded. He glanced at April and smiled shyly.

As David went back to speak to Barbara, April came up by his side and slid her hand just for a secret moment into his. She looked anxiously at him. Tony was relieved because she still wanted to touch him even though she was beautiful now. He smiled at her and quite suddenly all the weight of the day fell from him. It was all right. Everything was all right. He seemed to be watching everything – his mother sailing along, David sauntering by her with his hand in a pocket chatting away, the village, the river, the water – from a space somewhere deep inside himself. The space was long and deep and it was warm to its furthest corners. Everything was fine ... in fact, better than it would have been had David been a man in a suit with a car or a carriage and three polished horses. It was new, it was refreshing, informal. He was a bit eccentric, but nice. Like his mother in her boiler-suit.

The truth was, none of it was important anyway. Tony had a secret. April, beautiful April, wanted him as he wanted her. A rosy film unrolled over him, over the street, over Barbara and David, over the whole world. He had eyes only for April. He kept glancing at her the whole time, watching her move, watching her step carefully over the puddles and tip her head to one side as if she was listening. When he looked and she was watching him in the same way, they both smiled in delight. Tony wanted to lean across and touch her or kiss her or hold her, somehow to say, 'I'm here with you, now . . .' Of course he couldn't here in public, but just before they entered the tea-room he secretly touched her wrist with his fingers. It was like a stranger's wrist in the small white glove Barbara had lent her, but it was April who turned and smiled at him with pure pleasure before she ducked her head and stamped in through the door.

April put on her best table manners in the café. By this time she could eat like a princess, or would have done were it not for the noise. She was learning to feel the noises she made, but she was still oblivious to much of it. She would lift her cup to her lips like a humming bird approaching a blossom, and then suck the hot tea like faulty plumbing. Her cup would float through air back to its saucer like a chiffon scarf, but then crash down with such a crack you thought it might break. The other diners peered round anxiously. April waved her hand in the air at them and smiled proudly.

She was taking a great shine to David who, like her, had an enthusiasm for nature. He insisted they sit in a window seat so he could watch the outside world as they ate and pointed out the birds that flew past – a fly catcher darting out of the wisteria growing on a wall opposite, a duck that settled on the pavement, the martins and swallows that swooped along the street.

'House martins,' he observed. April shook her head disapprovingly.

'No?' enquired David. 'Sand martins, then?' April nodded enthusiastically and pointed down the river.

'You know their nests?' said David enthusiastically. 'We must see . . . what do you say, Barbara, shall we take a walk after tea?'

'I'm scarcely dressed . . .' declined Barbara politely.

'Oh, 'e onee us a i'le way . . .' April suddenly began explaining in a loud incoherent voice that it was just up round the corner. In the café, the rattle of knives and forks stopped as everyone peered round. But April, in near silence, heard nothing and talked on.

'What's she saying?' begged David.

'It's just a little way up the river,' translated Tony. He was beginning to get the knack of hearing her. She left out the consonants; if you remembered that it wasn't so hard. But he kicked her gently under the table. He was horribly embarrassed by her voice. Everyone was looking.

Armed with April's promise that it was just a little way, David pressed Barbara to come and she agreed, even though she secretly suspected that April's idea of a little way was not going to be hers. She felt most uncomfortable picking her way along the footpath, past the damp patches to keep her slender white shoes clean and watching the long grass and twigs deposit little collections of dirt and mud on her pristine snowy dress and pearly stockings. April walked ahead with David, pointing out clumps of interesting flowers or signs of wildlife. Tony was put out by the way April was taking to the stranger, and by the way the stranger seemed so unimpressed by his mother's efforts on his behalf. He walked behind with his mother and tried not to feel cross.

The martins nested in the sandy bank of a tributary of the main river. When April stamped on the bank, the little brown birds flew out like gunshot and soared out over the river. Soon, David, Tony and April were running over the tell-tale holes and stamping away to make them fly out, while Barbara waited patiently on a dry patch of cropped turf.

April suddenly grabbed David's hand and pointed to a dense bed of reeds growing along one edge of the tributary. She flapped her arms to indicate a bird.

'Reed buntings?' enquired David. 'Tits? Herons?' April was prancing about in excitement that she might have found an adult to share in one of her favourite pastimes. Suddenly her forearm shot out in front of her in a vivid mime. It was all there in her arm, the long writhing body, the quick head . . .

'Eels!' shouted David. 'Do you hear that, Barbara? Eels in that reed bed. We can catch our dinner!'

Barbara did her best to smile. It was obvious what was coming. Tony looked at his mother in her once white dress, now spattered with mud and streaked with dirt. Her face had gone hard and flinty and just for a second he hated April. April knew something was wrong. She was staring at Barbara's face, too, trying to work out what the matter was. David, however, was oblivious. Already he was sitting down pulling off his boots. Barbara smiled as warmly as she could at April.

'Please feel free,' she said. There was no trace of sarcasm or anger in her voice and David turned and smiled back. But April, excited from so much talk, was far more sensitive than any hearing person to the expression of a face and she saw clearly enough that Barbara was incensed. She paused uncertainly.

'Come on, April . . .' David tugged her dress. April sighed, but she couldn't resist the chance to show off to David. She sat down and began pulling off her shoes. Then she stood up and started stuffing her skirt into her knickers.

Unable to contain herself, Barbara hissed violently

and Tony nudged April with his foot. Barbara nodded at her legs and April stared in shocked amazement at her thighs, transformed from her usual brown, scratched, dirty pins into long lady's legs, encased in silk and suspenders. She blushed furiously and dashed away behind a hedge. She emerged a second later and thrust the stockings and suspender belt into Barbara's hand before she carried on where she had left off, energetically stuffing her dress into her long knicker legs. Thus prepared she and David began wading their way out to try and find the eels in the reed bed.

Back on the bank, Barbara unclicked her handbag and tucked the articles of underwear away out of sight. She glanced at Tony and pursed her lips.

Tony watched the two figures making their way to the reed bed. He was furious at the way April had taken to the newcomer, even though he knew it was ridiculous to be jealous of a man so much older than he was. As for Barbara, she was not used to being abandoned and upstaged by the likes of April Dean and she showed it. Little white lines of fury appeared by her nostrils.

'Is he . . . is he always like this?' asked Tony.

'Always, I forgot,' muttered Barbara. She sighed and looked down at her dress. Pristine, it had been stunning. Soiled, it looked like a rag. 'It's my own fault,' she groaned. 'I told myself to dress up in tweeds or something, but I cracked at the last minute.' She sighed again and gazed at the two figures stalking the reed bed. 'April,' she groaned. 'Look at her! All my good work. My dress! Oh, my poor dress.' Tony winced and stared after her. The dress had become untucked and was trailing in the water. David began making gestures to April but she thought he'd spotted something behind and went splashing away after his pointing fingers. David

shrugged, waved awkwardly at the shore and got back
to the search.

Barbara waved back enthusiastically, smiling at David
and groaning softly, 'No, no, no . . .' as she did it.

'Ay . . .!' There was a sudden shout from the reeds.
April dived down and groped about her feet in the
water, and then with a cry of triumph she held up
the long shining black fish. It wriggled and thrashed in
her hands.

'Well done!' bellowed David. 'Eels for tea . . .' He
began running as fast as he could to help her, splashing
like a hippopotamus through the knee deep water. But
the black shape in April's hands writhed and twisted
and dropped suddenly into the water. There followed a
frantic chase, during which he and April drenched each
other and nearly knocked one another flying before they
cornered the fish by the bank and bore it triumphantly
in the air. David ceremoniously opened the little rucksack he carried on his back and popped it in.

'Come on, quick . . . we need all the hands we can
get!' He waved to Barbara and Tony, begging them to
come over, although he obviously never thought they
would because he turned away at once. He and April,
who had done this many times before and was overjoyed
to find a fellow hunter, began walking slowly through
the water, feeling with their toes for the sudden squirm
of an eel under them in the mud.

'That looks like fun.' Tony watched them enviously.
But he didn't want to desert his mother.

'This has gone far enough.' Barbara suddenly got to
her feet as if she had made up her mind.

'What?' said Tony in alarm. 'Them?'

'No, us.' Barbara kicked off her shoes. She surrep-
titiously undid her own stockings, glancing anxiously up

and down the path as she did so, unrolled them and popped them with April's in her handbag. She took a few steps to the muddy water's edge. 'The dress will just have to meet a sticky end,' she sighed. She carefully dipped her toes into the water, let them sink into the mud. She giggled. 'It tickles!' she exclaimed. From the river, David and April turned and stared.

'Yoo-hoo, I'm coming ... save some for me,' she yodelled, and wobbled dangerously as her foot found a stone.

April shrieked. David stepped gallantly forward to offer her his hand. Poor Tony, still stuck on the bank, was suddenly subjected to all his old terrors. He froze with embarrassment and rage at her for humiliating him like this. But only for a moment. He wasn't going to be left out, he told himself fiercely ... he wasn't going to be left out ever again. He kicked off his shoes, rolled his trousers up and waded in after her.

Catching eels was the most fun ever. You had to squelch through the mud in your bare feet, feeling with your toes for the sudden electric squirm of the slippery fish as it dashed out from under you. That was just the start, because then you had to chase it through the shallow water. You could see them zipping along among the reeds and you dashed and splashed like an idiot after them. It seemed impossible but April was an expert and caught two more quite quickly. David and Tony lost theirs one after the other. In the end Tony fell over and got wet from tip to toe. After that he gave up trying to keep dry and the next time he found an eel he simply fell on it. But it still escaped.

As for Barbara, the first time she felt the eel under her toes she shrieked and leapt into the air and would have gone right in if David hadn't been nearby to catch her. Even so, she dipped her bottom in. After that she was hampered with trying to keep her bottom hidden. She had no idea what it looked like all wet, but no one else was going to find out either.

They had four eels in an hour, all caught by April. David slipped them into the knapsack he still carried on his back. Just then there was a noise from the bank. Looking up, Barbara saw to her horror the stunned faces of Mr and Mrs Riley. They were dressed in their Sunday best clothes, stiff and black and buttoned up to the nostrils. They were staring at her. Barbara stared back.

For a second she thought she would scream. She bit back the scream but tears of shame and frustration welled up in her eyes. The bank was twenty yards away and she was an utter disgrace. She was suddenly aware that she was wet through front and back. She was wearing a slip and the material of her dress was very far from see-through but even so it was far from decent. She was all too aware of Mr Riley's greedy, nasty eyes seeking out the contours of her body and underwear under the cloth.

If the bank had been a little nearer Barbara was certain she would have burst into tears and flounced back to dry land, splashing and falling like a brat in a tantrum. But with a great effort, her dignity got the better of her.

'Good afternoon, Mr Riley, Mrs Riley,' she called, as if she were speaking across the lawn at a posh tea party. 'We're catching our dinner. Would you care to join us?'

Behind her, David quickly hauled a writhing eel out of his bag. He held it in the air and smiled.

Mrs Riley huffed and turned away. Mr Riley paused, stared one lingering last look at Barbara before he turned and followed his wife reluctantly up the path.

Barbara turned her head back to the water and began treading after eels again. No one said anything, but her feelings were obvious. Her face had turned a bright, painful red.

Shortly after that they packed up and went back. Barbara sent Tony on ahead to get her cloak so she could get safely and decently through the village. In the house, with the eels in the sink and the fire going, a cup of hot chocolate in her hand and wrapped safely up in a nice thick gown, Barbara began to remember Riley's face as he ogled her and she began to laugh and laugh and laugh . . .

Later, when everyone had gone home, Barbara had a long hot bath. Two eels writhed in the kitchen sink for April to prepare the next day. Tony had walked April home in the dark and they had hidden in the bushes by her house and kissed and kissed until they were both drunk. That was the best thing of all. That, and the fact that his mother was capable of anything, anything she wanted, because she had turned a disaster into a festival yet again.

Tony was sure that his mother had had just as wonderful a time as he had. So it was with great surprise, when she at last went to bed after him that Tony heard, very distinctly through the walls, the sound of his mother weeping.

Tony need not have worried so much about his mother. She had indeed had a wonderful time splashing about in the reeds, feeling the mud between her toes. When she had nearly fallen in and David caught her and held her close to him it was like old times, twenty years ago when they had been sweet on each other. But as she

111

had dressed that morning, she had allowed herself to think she might be able to recapture her old life of wealth and elegance when she went out for tea in the afternoon. Lying in bed, the mud on her dress, the dreadful humiliation of the Rileys seeing her drenched and muddy, and the general collapse of her life had overcome her. The new life was coming on rather too fast and she wept that night for all the good things she had lost.

The next morning, Barbara felt a good deal brighter. While Tony was at work with the odious Riley, a posy of tulips arrived from David together with a telegram in which he impressed her with how very much he had enjoyed so many wonderful things the day before, the most wonderful, of course, being Barbara herself. 'You always rise to the occasion,' he remarked.

Barbara smiled wanly. It was true. She was always capable of rising to the occasion, even if, as on this occasion, she had no choice. But if the poor dear man had known what it cost her . . .!

The arrival of the telegram interrupted her reading a rather more important letter, a letter Barbara had hidden from Tony and kept until he was at work. Now, with her tulips in water and the appreciative telegram tucked into the toast rack, Barbara took the letter from her pocket and opened it. The letter was from her husband.

Elliot made it as clear as he could that she could expect no reconciliation and not very much help. He regretted this. He said he could not afford two households and felt that he owed it to the woman he loved to provide for her first. He would be willing to offer a little more, however . . . But there were conditions. She must grant him a divorce, she must agree to his terms and, first of all, she must remove the pressure she had put on him at work. The directors had obviously been asking questions. Barbara smiled and took a quick sip of tea. Her appetite, which the waiting letter had killed, was returning.

She finished reading, took off her reading glasses and popped the letter into her pocket. Barbara had no intention of accepting his terms, terms which weren't even defined. Nor had she any intention of stopping the pressure. Her husband had up till now refused even to acknowledge her letters. The fact that he was now replying showed that the pressure was working.

What Barbara wanted was no less than . . . everything. Everything back. She wanted her house, her servants, her income, the school for her boy, the same standard of living, everything. If he wanted a mistress, let him keep her as he was trying to keep his wife and son. She was prepared to go that far. She would act out the good wife and go with him to the social evenings and dances and dinners where the bank expected its employees to bring their wives and show off their families. She would not ask questions when he didn't come home at night or spent time away. She made no claims on his heart. But financially she would give no quarter. She wanted everything back. She would get everything.

As for David, Barbara wasn't sure how much she believed in old romances, or even in love itself for that matter. She had loved him . . . once. She was still very fond of him and had only accepted his help because her plight was desperate and because he insisted he only wanted the chance to help an old and dear friend. The problem with David was, she thought, leaning back in her chair as she considered her options . . . the trouble was, he could not really afford her. All the other things – the fact that he preferred to get his hands dirty than

go to the theatre, the fact that he dressed like a trades-
man and didn't care a hoot about who worried about it
– all that was difficult but not impossible. It was even
refreshing. Barbara was adaptable. Once, she had loved
him for being like that. Maybe she could again, but she
was not sure that she wanted to. She had her own style.
And her style was an expensive business.

If he had really wanted, much could have been made
of that bicycle business. But David was simply unin-
terested in getting rich. When he should have been
employing workers and expanding his business, he got
stuck in the workshops building new bicycles because he
liked it. Barbara ruled nothing out. She hoped that
he hoped, but she did not hope herself. She was not sure
she wanted to fall in love again, but even if she did she
would certainly not be foolish enough to let that prevent
her from getting all that she deserved from her husband.
David would never be well off. That was why she had
not married him when he asked her all those years ago,
even though she had loved him. And it was still true.

All in all, Barbara considered she was making good
progress in what she called her manoeuvres. Her husband had decided to sever all communications; she had
forced him to communicate. She would force further.
She would write that very morning while Tony was at
work to urge her contacts to increase the pressure. If
she wanted, Barbara considered she could cost her husband his job. She was prepared to do that but doubtless
it would not be necessary. And in the meantime there
was David and a long summer which she was going to
do her best to enjoy to the full.

Barbara said nothing of all this to Tony. He had no
idea of her plans or actions against her husband and she
had no intention of telling him. She considered that

114

she had made a mistake in telling him about his father's mistress at all. When he came back that afternoon he was in a temper and after some prompting, revealed that it was Riley. He had been nagging him to get her to pay back the money they owed, he claimed, but Barbara suspected it was more than that. She knew Riley's kind. No doubt he would be spreading it about the village as fast as he could that Barbara Piggot had spent Sunday afternoon splashing about in the reeds with a man friend with her legs bare and her dress wet. He would have been very busy indeed, she considered, with his own little embroideries . . . busy dragging her through the mud.

'Perhaps you'd better pack the job in then, darling,' Barbara said carelessly so he wouldn't know how much she hated the thought of Riley gossiping about her. Tony was jubilant. The next morning his mother went down to pay off her debts to Riley with money taken from the jar in the crockery cupboard, and to tell him that her son wouldn't be needing the job any longer. She was very cool with the grocer, who had obviously been taking advantage of her boy. Riley noted it. Tony was relieved to get away but they had made an enemy.

And now for Tony, everything was set. The new house was perfect, they had money, they had friends. Everything was changing and everything new was better than anything old. His mother was invincible. It didn't matter that she delayed longer than he wanted in getting rid of Uncle Bob, or that she used her charms to winkle favours out of the likes of Riley. She was capable of anything. Once she had seemed beautiful, distant and without purpose. Now she was a house around him. David was nice, too. He came every weekend, took them

115

out, treated them. April showed him round the estuary and quickly came to be very fond of him. Barbara didn't make the same mistake of dressing up for cocktails when they were going out for the day, and in return he took her out every now and then to somewhere where she really could dress for cocktails. Every weekend he set homework for Tony and April. Tony never bothered with it, but April took care to do it as well as she could and David was very impressed by her quick mind and her willingness to learn.

'She could be anything, with the right sort of education,' he told Barbara.

Tony liked the new man. He liked the way he seemed to open up his mother still further and fitted in so neatly with their new way of being. He knew that David and his mother had once been sweethearts. Without really thinking about it, Tony came to assume that they would become so again. One day they would marry and this new life, which had become so much better in every way than the old one, would go on forever.

That was the outer world; April was the world within.

10

These were the golden days, the idyllic weeks. When they were alone it was different from anything else – an undiscovered country. It could be brought to life at any moment – by April suddenly leaning up and breathing in his ear, by the smell of dusky liquorice on her breath, by him sliding his hands under her clothes, by lying hidden in the grass, watching the little fishing boats sailing up and down the water, and kissing and exposing her skin to the sun.

Sometimes, boating on the river early in the morning or at dusk when the mist rose from the water, April would tip the oars and let them drift. It was still on the river at such times. The distant noises of the land . . . birds singing, horses neighing, the chug, chug, chug of a car or boat, all seemed enveloped in stillness. The stillness was so deep Tony sometimes felt he could hear it if he listened hard enough. The silence was the river or the mist but it was also April. At the heart of her, hidden by her noisy deafness and the ignorance of the villagers, was a still, quiet place that he was approaching. He would lean over the side of the boat and watch her face, keeping very still and listening. If he listened closely enough, he would hear her true voice.

It was a secret. Inside the world they lived and moved in was a whole other world, there only for them. They carried this secret inside them like a deep well, a long, dark cavern inside that had never been there before. They were aware of it all the time; it was like a joke that no one else seemed to know. Tony loved to kiss her in the parlour when his mother was next door, to fill the room with them and see his mother come back in and know nothing. When they were alone together on the river about some activity, all Tony ever had to do was lean across and breathe warmly in her crippled ear. Then April would drop her rod or the oars and just stop and kiss him . . . in the boat, on the bank, lying in the grass, standing waist deep in the cool river. Then everything went still – the birds singing, the grasshoppers, the sounds of the boatyard and the village in the distance – everything hung in the air, waiting for them to come back. Then something would move and they would part and glide slowly back into the world around them.

The world where they fell in love was April's world, the world of the water, the tide in the estuary, the swans living in a kennel outside her door, the fishing, the islands. April felt that she was growing up at last, but losing nothing. She had always thought of the grown-up world, the real world, as a grim, hard place. But now she was learning to behave and at the same time her own world was growing bigger. Now there were kisses and touching and wanting someone to know everything about her, everything about her world. She had a boy-friend, like Jenny. One day – and she had never believed this before – she would get married and have children like the other girls. But her children would be different, because she would teach them the secret world inside that none of the others knew.

Tony would have kept it a secret from everyone and forever, but there were other reasons for this. He was ashamed of April. She wasn't in his class. She was deaf, not right. He would be teased and expected to treat her differently. She wasn't the sort of person he wanted; she wasn't the sort of person who ought to be able to make him feel like this. But she did, and for that reason he

118

was ashamed of himself, too. Later, when this holiday was over, it might be different. He might boast to his school friends how she had let him do what he liked to her. So he imagined, but he could not imagine describing how it felt when they walked out and the last houses of the village vanished behind the trees, and he took her hand and smiled at her because they were under a spell.

But April was in a hurry. She was giving herself to him, but where was his world? That was the world she wanted to join and Tony was her passport. He never said anything and always let go of her hand when anyone was near, but there was no mistaking the magic bubble around them. She was so proud that Tony wanted to be with her, that the world went warm when he touched her, that he had fallen for her, the deaf mute, the village idiot. With Tony, unlike all the others, she was an equal. Sooner or later, April would become impatient. She wanted him to show her off, to hold her hand as they walked through the village, to put his arm around her when they sat in the parlour in front of his mother. Sooner or later . . . but it never got that far.

Two weeks after Tony packed in his job, Mrs Dean came over to have a talk with Barbara. She was worried about her daughter and Tony. It wasn't right for a boy and girl of that age to spend so much time together unsupervised. Who knows what they got up to, alone out there?

Barbara had of course noticed what was going on. Well, why not? Boys will be boys. If he wanted to fool around it was better to fool around with April than with someone who really mattered. So far her only concern was that Tony didn't get too involved. She'd warned him as much but he'd stared at her as if she was talking gibberish. At the time she thought it was embarrassment.

Mrs Piggot liked April; she was grateful to her and when she was out of this mess she fully intended to do something to help her. But Barbara's grandfather had been a lord. April and her mother were working people and they were almost another species as far as she was concerned. Even so, she didn't want it to get out of hand. Fooling about was one thing, but she didn't want the girl getting into trouble – she could do without that on top of everything.

She consulted David about it that weekend.

'But they're both so young!' he objected.

'Not too young to get into trouble,' commented Barbara. She rubbed her lip. 'April's rather backward in some ways but very forward in others. She's a bit too used to getting what she wants.'

'That won't do her any harm,' said David. 'It would be a pity to stop them seeing each other,' he added after a moment's thought. 'It's doing her no end of good having someone like Tony taking her seriously. She adores him, you can see it. And after all the help she's given you . . . She'd be very hurt.'

'Yes,' agreed Barbara. 'And so might Tony.'

The conversation didn't reassure her. She had assumed it was just playing around, Tony making the most of his summer off. But . . . 'They're in love,' she realised with a shock. And that would never do, because sweet though April was, she was not the sort of person she expected her son to fall for. Her mother was a char, for Heaven's sake! But she had left it too late. She could hardly stop them seeing each other now.

She had another word with Tony and charged him with going too far. But Tony denied that they had even kissed.

Mrs Dean was taken aback when she heard. 'Perhaps they're just children, after all,' she sighed.

Barbara snorted. It was obvious! The whole village could see it. So what were they hiding?

What they were hiding was themselves. Barbara and Mrs Dean need not have worried about that. April and Tony had not made love . . . not yet. April was very proud at how sensible she was being. She wore trousers and her bra when they were out together, as her mother advised. Neither of them wanted to go all the way. Even when they lay wrapped in their towels after a swim and embraced and suddenly found themselves skin to skin, one or the other always pulled back. They were so involved with each other that they were actually surprised when their mothers spoke to them, they hardly believed that anyone else knew. After that they behaved with more caution, but only for a while.

Barbara was right. The whole village knew. The village had known all along and brooded on it for three weeks – those idyllic weeks.

It began like so many of their days with a walk by the river. They went together, past the woodyard, past the trees, beyond the boatyard. When they left the path they held hands.

It was Saturday, two o'clock. They'd just had lunch with Barbara and David. David had a treat to announce. Tomorrow they would all go to the regatta, April too. April was delighted. Tomorrow she would go to the regatta and be a lady. Somehow, she would always be a lady now. Tony and Mrs Piggot and David would talk to her and take her seriously, treat her as if she was one of them. Perhaps behind the tent, or when no one was looking, Tony would touch her lightly on the neck, or

121

her hand, or briefly slide his fingers between the buttons at the back of her dress. The real world, the secret world, all together.

Tony was not so pleased. It was a waste of a day. He could go to the regatta any time . . . would again, when this holiday was over. He was bothered about being seen out with April. And he was bothered about the way his mother made April behave – posh dresses, make-up, manners like a duchess. That wasn't April! Sometimes he thought his mother was just amusing herself. If she really wanted to help April she would have taught her to type or sew or read better or write, something useful. But the exercises in the evenings had tailed away altogether by now and there was only the work David gave her at weekends. What would happen to her when they left? She would be just as she was, except that she could eat a cucumber sandwich better than anyone else in the village. He had heard David say as much to his mother. But his mother lacked the patience and concentration to teach such basic skills, so she fell back on the only real accomplishments she had – how to eat a cucumber sandwich nicely. And confidence.

They walked along in silence . . . just walking and waiting to find a place to swim, or sit or picnic.

They sat for a while on an old brick ruin half broken up by trees and drank cordial from a bottle. They had sandwiches but it was too early. Then they got up and walked on. They had gone maybe two or three hundred yards when April remembered . . . the cordial bottle. She mimed drinking from the bottle and pointed back. They'd left it behind. She ran back quickly along the path to fetch it while he waited alone.

122

Tony moved closer to the river and sat down. Some birds were singing but it was very quiet. April was a long time. When he heard someone coming towards him along the footpath he got up; he hated meeting other people on these outings. But it was too late. A boy, a young man, four or five years older than him, came along the path towards him. He had seen him in the town. Tony tried to leave quietly but the lad called him.

'On your own, are you?' called the boy. Tony looked back down the river where April had gone. The boy came close and Tony nodded . . . yes, on his own.

The boy stood next to him with his hands in his pockets and watched Tony closely. He didn't look friendly. He nodded at the little knapsack by his side, the knapsack in which they'd forgotten to put the bottle back. 'Picnic?' he said.

'Sandwiches,' said Tony. He glanced down the river. He was anxious lest April come back. The boy glanced down river. They looked at each other. Behind them a blackbird called out an alarm. In the silence that followed Tony could hear the soft noise the river mud made when the tide went out, the sound of the water draining out of it back down to the river.

The boy said suddenly, 'You better go home now.' Tony looked up in alarm. The boy took a couple of steps and stood right next to him. Their clothes were almost touching. 'You leave her alone, right?' the boy said.

'What?'

'You know. The dummy. Hanging around with her. You mind your own business.'

The boy was getting angry. Tony took a step back. He looked back after her, where she had disappeared.

'I don't know . . .' he stammered.

'You've been mucking around with her. Taking her

123

for a ride. You and your mum. Dressing her up like a monkey.' He was repeating the village gossip. 'Leave off, right?'

Tony stared away. How did they know? It was awful that they knew.

'Scram!' The boy was pulling an ugly face. He was getting ready to fight. 'You leave her alone from now on,' said the boy again, and he jerked his head in the direction of the village.

Tony mechanically picked up his knapsack and took a few steps. He paused. He wanted to ask where she was but he didn't dare.

'She's with us now. We'll take care of her. She wants you to get lost. She knows what's going on, now. She's had enough of you. Get it?'

Tony nodded and walked quickly away. He stumbled on the grass edges of the footpath. When he looked back the boy was still watching him. He walked until he was out of sight.

They knew. They thought like that about it. Tony stumbled along the path chaotically. They knew ... everyone knew. April had told him to get lost. She was going off with them now. He remembered what Riley had said, how she used to hang about with boys, three at a time, he'd said. Tony had never asked April about it, he'd barely thought about it since then. Now it all came back and it seemed to make sense. She used to do things with them. When he came she'd done them with him. Now she was bored with him and she was going with them again.

Although it really seemed like that to him he wanted to see for himself and be certain. The thing with leaving the bottle behind was a trick of hers to get rid of him.

She'd been playing with him. But he turned round. After a second, when he was sure the boy wasn't near, he left the path and began to creep back.

April had shared everything with Tony . . . but not Tad and Joe. How could she? She was too scared – scared that to speak it made it more real, scared too, that it would get between them. It wasn't the sort of thing that happened to nice girls. She knew what the village thought of her, she knew what sort of girl showed herself to two or three boys at a time on the river bank, willingly or unwillingly. She didn't want Tony to think of her like that. She wanted the whole thing to be a black dream and so she had never said.

Behind the old brick building was a hollow, overgrown with young trees. They dragged her here. They kept quiet, and Tony might have stumbled among them if they'd stayed quiet. But Tad laughed jeeringly and Joe said, 'Hairy cow, isn't she?' His voice sounded almost tearful. Tony froze. He was too near! He turned and crept away and when he was sure they wouldn't hear his feet on the brittle leaves and twigs, he crept round behind the hollow and climbed a little way up a tree, so that he could spy down.

They were half hidden in the bushes. She lay on the ground, they crouched around her. Her blouse was open, her bra rucked up under her neck. They were touching her. He could see her trousers hanging off a bush. She just lay there, letting them.

It was true. She was letting them do that . . . things more boldly than he had ever done. They were peering at her, watching their hands, watching each other. They squabbled like gulls. She was letting them as she had let him and it was horrible. Tony's heart was beating like a

125

drum and it seemed it had always been true but he couldn't tear himself away.

Then suddenly it changed. April tried to sit up and there were three hard, rapid blows. He could see it all. One of them struck her stomach. One of them shoved her back down hard. And as April began to scream Tad slapped his hand over her mouth with a clap. There was a vicious, whispered threat and another hard slap. And then it was all the same scene again; but different. This was violence.

In the shock of realising what was happening, and the relief that she was still his after all, and the shame that he had failed her and his terrible fear for her, Tony forgot the boys and screamed . . .

'April! . . . April!'

Birds crashed out of the trees by him. He saw two faces, oval, white with fright, looking up. He saw April roll to one side. Then he was letting himself fall out of the tree and he was running, running, crashing through the bushes, through the brambles, running away before they got him too. He half crouched as he ran to keep out of sight because, of course, they'd have to silence him now. He zig-zagged and cut through the undergrowth to escape.

At last he couldn't go on any more and found a ditch to hide in. His heart was burning. There was his ragged breath and the birds, unconcerned, singing in the distance. After a few minutes he got up but he had no idea of what to do. Back to her? They might be waiting. Home? They might be waiting. But what of April? Had they just carried her away somewhere else, where they wouldn't be disturbed this time? Tony was ashamed and frightened. In the end he began to make his way back to the brick building. After hovering around for endless wasted minutes, he decided no one was there and went to explore. There, overlooking the river where they had stopped, was the half-full bottle of cordial. But down below in the hollow among the saplings there was nothing.

Tony began on his way home. They might be waiting for him but he had to get home and tell his mother, Mrs Dean, someone. Once he was in the village he would be all right. He hoped his cry had saved April, he hoped she was home this minute because otherwise it would be going on again and what could he do this time?

He found her a hundred yards further on ... or she found him. She had hidden herself in the bushes by the footpath and ran out when she saw him.

'Did they rape you?' begged Tony.

April shook her head. She clung to him and wept and wept. She was shaking with fear and shame. It was two hours before she consented to let him take her home. She'd thought she was another person now but she was just the same to them.

11

Don't tell, don't tell on me, don't tell anyone. April's voice soared and cracked. Tony was confused. It was as if the knowledge in other people's minds of what had been done to her was worse than the acts themselves – as if she had done something wrong.

'But they might do it again!' he begged. April panicked and wept; no one must ever know. Tony didn't understand but he couldn't argue.

The threat against April had only just begun. She knew, had known for a long time, that as far as the village was concerned the problem was not the boys and what they did, but who they did it to. Would they have attacked Jenny or any other of the young girls who walked the village and the river bank? Certainly not. The village would think April had turned the boys to this. The information was dangerous not to them, but to her.

Now the secret was different. No one must ever know. The next day at the regatta they went along as if everything was the same. April felt naked in the crowd. Tony watched her as if she might fall apart. Once he stood behind her and slid his fingers secretly in between the buttons on the back of her dress. April tensed violently and glanced back at him, a curious look of horror. He dropped his hand and looked away.

The fact was when he touched her she didn't think of him any more, or of days on the river and kisses in the boat. She thought of two boys holding her down on the damp mud and mauling her. They had put a spell on her, they had burned themselves into her. A touch, a kiss, a hand on her skin and what came to life? There at the heart of the secret, where April and Tony had been, were Tad and Joe.

After the regatta when she got home April boiled water and sat in the tin bath in the scullery for an hour. 'What are you doing, you don't need another one already, for God's sake!' scolded her mother. April had done the same thing the night before. She could not get clean enough. This was how she felt, that someone had spat inside her heart. The next day she and Tony went out together and it got worse. Something had died and he could only watch.

April wanted it kept quiet but she would have been better to have spoken out. She couldn't bear to but Tad and Joe had no such problem.

When the two boys saw Tony fall out of the tree and run off, they were badly scared. They knew people had gone to jail for less than they had done. Now that April was friends with the likes of Mrs Piggot they could suffer for their fun. Despite this they were quite unable to keep their mouths shut. In fact, at the first telling of the good time he and his friend had had with April, boasting to some younger boys still at school, Tad had played down the fact that April had to be beaten and held down before she would submit. In his telling, April enjoyed it . . . encouraged it. And as he spoke, he realised that boasting after all was his best defence.

That was how it began. Once they saw that they were actually making it safe for themselves by talking, the two lads spread the word as fast as they could. Cibblesham village did the rest. Everyone knew what April was like. These days she dressed in posh frocks and followed Mrs Piggot about the village with her little

129

finger cocked, but underneath she was the same as ever. It was like teaching a parrot to talk; she knew how to do things but not what they meant. Now she was dropping her knickers for Tony, for Joe, for Tad and no doubt half the other lads in the village as well. So what else was new? The poor little rich boy had been mooning about after her for the past few weeks; he'd be in for a shock when he discovered there was a queue going halfway round the village and back.

Riley did his bit. People called for their shopping, went away knowing a little more – or thinking they did. When you thought about it, he said, leaning forward and speaking softly, Mrs Dean and Mrs Piggot, two single women trying to bring up their children with no men – it was bound to turn sour. No school for the boy. The girl had been half wild ever since her father died. Both of them running about unsupervised, spending the day together by the river. Something was bound to happen. And that Mrs Piggot was a terrible flirt; no wonder her husband left her. Why, she'd been in the village no more than two weeks when she started up with that man from the bicycle shop in Redcliffe! No one was so innocent as to think he paid for that nice little house in the main street for free, surely . . .? If the mothers were like that, the children were bound to turn out worse. And see how it was affecting the local lads! Well, boys will be boys, but it was wrong all the same. Something would have to be done.

Others were more sympathetic to April. It wasn't her fault. But they could all see how it would end. She'd get pregnant. The baby would be put up for adoption and April would go into care, where, if the truth were told, she should have been these past four or five years. Sterilisation was the only real answer because even if they locked her up she'd find a way with the other inmates, no doubt. No one could accuse her of being fussy. So sad. But what could you do with people like that? She wasn't able to look after herself, let alone a baby.

These were not idle threats. Where was the place in the world for April? In that age there were no hearing aids, which would have transformed her life. There were places, special schools that could have taught her to earn her living, but they were far beyond the means of Mrs Dean. April was learning fast, but late, and the wrong things. This was a world where to be incapable was to be mad. No one was going to feed and clothe April because she could eat her dinner like a lady. The doctor in the village would not need a lot of persuading to certify her insane ... her morals, her behaviour, everything pointed to it. Even if he didn't think she was insane what else was there? Sterilisation to protect her from herself, four walls to protect society ... There were all too few solutions available to April.

As the gossip turned ugly, the mood got angry. People were angry at April for bringing this scandal to the village, angry at the boys for their stupidity and for taking advantage of the girl's innocence. Sensing what they were about to do to April, they looked around for someone to blame. That wasn't difficult.

Of course, it could have all been different if it wasn't for the newcomers. How they had taken advantage of the poor halfwit! The mother used her as an unpaid servant, worked her fingers to the bone for nothing, while the boy took her out and did what he liked in the afternoon as if she were his private whore. And all she got out of it was to play dressing-up once a week, like a bear at a picnic while they laughed at her behind her back . . .

Of course Barbara heard none of this. Riley smiled and scraped when she came to do her shopping. The other villagers greeted her politely when they met in the street; some of them touched their hats deferentially. She was still a lady no matter what. But she noticed people weren't as friendly as they had been. Then on Friday, the vicar turned up at Mrs Dean's house in the evening to have a word. Did she know that April was fooling about with the village boys again? It had seemed things were getting better while the Piggots took up with her; it would be a pity to let things slip . . .

After he left, Helen Dean ran upstairs and demanded an explanation. April feigned inability to understand.

'You know what I'm talking about,' shouted her mother, enraged that all the progress was falling away again. 'Do you want the whole village to know you're a slut?' She banged the door. April wept, but she would never tell her mother the truth. It was better, and somehow in her mind closer to the truth, that it had never happened.

Mrs Dean went round to tell Barbara about the visit. Barbara promised to do all she could but privately thought there was little she could do. Mrs Dean had not done a good job with the child. A pity, but if April wanted to do favours for the village boys no one could stop her. She only hoped Tony wouldn't be too hurt when he found out.

The next morning she told him that the vicar was worried about April's welfare and asked him to keep an eye out for what she was up to when she wasn't with him. He would find out sooner or later what but she didn't want to be the one to tell him. Tony looked suspiciously at her but didn't say anything.

That Sunday in church the vicar preached a sermon about the dangers of rumours and told the parable about Jesus saving the adulterous woman . . . 'Let him who has not sinned cast the first stone.' The villagers, who had been hoping for a sermon on loose morals, were not pleased. Many of the women – now mothers, grandmothers, wives – had in their own day hidden themselves by the river so that their boyfriends could open their clothes and touch them where they would. Now the boyfriends were husbands – the postmaster, the railway porter, the blacksmith, the labourer on the farm. They were all outraged. Were their wives to be put in the same class as April Dean, the deaf idiot who did it with anyone? It was generally agreed, the vicar had got it wrong.

Meanwhile the little glances, the strained conversations, the turned heads . . . Barbara was getting curious and irritated. Her son was anxious and fretted when April was away from him but he would admit nothing. The mood in the village was getting angrier. One day it came out into the open.

She was out with Tony, walking in the trees behind the village to pick flowers for the house and fir cones for the fire. Although it was summer she liked the smell and cosy atmosphere at night when she pulled the curtains and the bright fire jumped in the grate.

As they walked back onto the main street, a dray cart was being unloaded outside the Black Bull. The big shire horse stood calmly, his nose hidden in a nose bag. He tossed his head and chaff and corn spilled onto the road. The cellar was open and the drayman and the landlord were rolling the heavy beer barrels down the ramp into the cellar. The warm, bitter smell of beer wafted out of the ground and into the street.

The landlord's son, a boy a little older than Tony, stood by the dray helping steer the barrels towards the wooden ramp underground. He watched Tony and his mother walk past on the other side of the road. He seemed to be waiting for something. Tony kept his eyes on him and sure enough, the instant his mother turned her head to look the other way, the boy grinned at Tony and made an obscene gesture with his arm.

But the boy mis-timed badly. Barbara stopped dead in her tracks; the boy opposite froze. She had turned at the last second and seen everything. Nervously the boy began to edge himself behind the dray ... but down came his father's hand on his shoulder. He cringed and looked up at the landlord, expecting a blow.

Barbara stood coolly and watched. The boy deserved a cuff round the ear at least and she intended to see it done. The landlord shifted under her gaze. But then he looked back. For a second the two stood staring each other down. Then, he patted his boy on the shoulder and nodded slightly.

Barbara flushed red with rage and embarrassment. She glanced to each side to see who had witnessed this humiliation. Then she swung on her heel and marched Tony back home.

At first, Barbara thought the gesture must have been aimed at her; and she would have someone skinned alive for that. But as she thought about it she considered that on the whole, the boy was probably doing it for Tony.

She started on him as soon as she got home. Why had

the boy made that gesture? What had been going on? Was it anything to do with him and April . . .?

Tony stalled and hedged. He insisted he had no idea, the boy was just teasing him, it meant nothing. But the landlord hadn't backed up his boy for nothing.

Finally she said, 'Did you know that April has been hanging about the village boys? The vicar was complaining about it to her mother. You're not the only one, you know . . .'

'It wasn't like that!'

And now he began to talk. He wasn't sure if he was betraying or helping, but it had gone too far now and he was angry that April was being blackened in that way.

Barbara listened in horror. So it was like that! She might have known. When he finished she began firing more questions. Had they raped her? No, she said not. Had it happened before? Yes, she used to sleep away at the weekends to escape them. Sleep away? She hadn't been safe in her own home? So she said. Had he and April . . . slept together? No, never. But other things? Well, yes. How long for? Weeks . . . a month maybe. Then why on earth had he lied to her before when she asked? Because . . . it was a secret. Had they been seen? They used to think not but he supposed, reluctantly, that yes, they must have been seen . . .

Barbara began to pace up and down, up and down. She was furious. The stupid boy, the stupid, stupid boy! She had let things get badly out of hand. How all this must reflect on her, on her reputation as a mother, as a respectable woman. She knew how such little villages regarded outsiders. And April! Poor April. She thought she had been helping the girl . . .

She looked round at Tony staring anxiously at her, his white face. She knew what he wanted. She was to save April; the whole situation must be turned around. She was the one who knew how to change things. They had been penniless and she had pulled a life for them out of nowhere, a life better than the one that went before. But what was there up her sleeve this time?

'You've not been helping her, you know,' she told her son. 'Did you bother to think about her reputation?'

Tony looked away.

'The whole village must know . . .' seethed Barbara. She thought hatefully of the calm, grim nod from the landlord, of Riley spreading his insolent views from his gossip shop on the corner. To be the subject of this sort of talk from the common people! She continued pacing up and down, running a long finger nervously across her lower lip.

'It'll be all April's fault, of course, she'll be the one to suffer, you needn't worry about yourself,' she told Tony angrily.

'That's not fair!'

She turned to look at him. She knew; the gossip made everything different, crude, ugly. It hadn't been like that at the time. And yet, the gossip was real, reputation was real. Their little affair of the heart was fluff on the wind. Tomorrow it would be nothing.

'You're as bad as your father,' she said evenly. Tony sat slowly down on the table.

His mother began to bustle about, getting her shawl, her hat. 'Where are you going?' he asked.

'To see the vicar. He'll know how far things have gone. Vicars do.' She paused at the door. 'Where's April?'

'I don't know . . .' Tony couldn't explain how things

were between them. He hadn't seen much of her for a few days.

Barbara snorted in angry amusement. It was already over. Up the river with her latest beau, no doubt. She still thought that, despite what Tony said. 'If she comes round, send her away. Do you hear? For her own good . . .'

Tony nodded. She hurried up the street to the vicarage.

Barbara came back from the vicarage an hour later in a rather more thoughtful mood. The vicar was sympathetic . . . to her, to her son, to April. It was a sad case . . . an unnecessarily sad case. But sympathy only got you so far. The root of the problem remained: April.

'But didn't you tell him? Didn't you tell him she never wanted to . . . They were trying to rape her!'

His mother hung her shawl on the hook in the porch. She scratched her eyelid. 'Of course I did, but . . . It doesn't actually make so very much difference, dear,' she said.

Tony couldn't believe it. 'But you know what they're like here . . . you know what they think of April.'

Of course it was true. They all thought April was a halfwit when in fact she was a very clever and quick young girl . . . a bit too clever for her own good, in fact.

'We didn't know her before,' pointed out Barbara. 'Apparently . . . well, put it like this. No one is terribly surprised if these boys think they can do what they want with her . . .' She watched Tony, who shook his head. He couldn't understand why it was *April* who was in trouble.

'The vicar, like many men, has a great many morals but not much sense when it comes to women,' observed Barbara, sitting down at the table and folding her hands in front of her. 'They think our reputations are more important than we are. That's why they don't like us to think for ourselves, and that's why it's important that we do think for ourselves . . . which is what I've been trying to show April.' She said that to show her son that she was on their side, really. 'Unfortunately we all really do have to live by our reputations. That's not always fair, but it's a fact. And April has a reputation. It would be nice to remind them,' she added with a trace of bitterness, 'that she also has a soul.'

Barbara knew something of what April was going through. She had once had a similar experience herself. It had happened when she was sixteen, walking home on a footpath by a tall hedgerow from a friend's house. She'd thought she was all alone, every living soul safe inside. But suddenly out from nowhere in the darkness someone seized her and pulled her against his body. He tore open her bodice and put his hand inside and squeezed her neck hard with his other hand so she couldn't breathe properly. All this was terrifying, humiliating, disgusting. But the worst thing he did was to speak her name.

Barbara had fought back and got out a scream. The man had run off although he could easily have overpowered her. Perhaps he had already done all he wanted to do. But Barbara never forgot. Nearly thirty years on, the fear of that encounter still made her sweat, her heart beat, her feet hurry when the dusk came and she had a lonely place to walk. For months afterwards, whenever a man friend offered her his arm, or wanted to take her out, or merely stopped to talk, she wondered . . . was it you, was it you? Because he had known her; he said her name. Someone shared this secret with her. How often did he enjoy watching her watching him and wondering if it was he who had torn her dress and held her breast? She never found out who it was, though she had her suspicions. She could imagine the reign of terror April was living through now. She knew only too well what it was that had driven the girl to spend the cold winter nights on her island, where she was at least safe.

The hypocrisy made her sick. All the village gossiping because her boy had gone sweet on the poor child, as if it were some sin. How many of them had done the same thing? Why, the girl was being quite sensible . . . wearing trousers when she went off with Tony, hiding herself away from those boys. And still they got her. But . . . there was a lot that the vicar said that she agreed with. Mrs Dean had let April run wild. The girl had been allowed, and had allowed herself to become the object of lust. The result. . . she lived in terror and those two boys could find themselves in serious trouble. They could lose their jobs, they could get fined or even go to jail. Yes, the root of the problem was certainly April.

'Can I tell her . . . that you know?'

Barbara sighed and nodded. 'But you understand – all this has to stop, Tony? No more days out alone? You can see that?'

Tony frowned.

'No more being seen by the river together. No more . . . hanky-panky.'

He smiled uncertainly and ran down the road to find April.

All that week there had been a beast sitting between them. Perhaps now it would be different . . . his mother was on their side. But when she knew it was out, April hunched up in a ball and began to weep. She covered

her face with her hands and rocked to and fro and
moaned.

'But it was already out ... everybody knew, April,
everybody ...' insisted Tony. April continued to moan.
Tony put his arm awkwardly around her but she
remained hunched up in a ball against his stomach. Tony
was getting to understand more – how frightened she
was, how dangerous the information was to her – but he
didn't know everything. April hadn't told the truth. The
fact was, when he had found her trapped by the two
boys, he had after all been too late. She had been raped.
Tad had his go. Joe had been unable. She had no idea
herself why she couldn't tell. She felt so ashamed.

'They won't try anything again now that Mother's seen
the vicar,' said Tony. But April, her head buried in her
hands, cried and cried and wouldn't watch his face and
wouldn't know what he was saying.

That evening Barbara went across to see Mrs Dean. The
other woman listened in stunned silence to what she had
seen coming for years, but had lately convinced herself
would pass them by.

As Barbara talked, April's mother began to dissolve.
'But what can I do? What's to become of her, Mrs
Piggot?' she cried, her face screwing up in grief.

Barbara put her arm around her and tried to comfort
her. Helen Dean watched her between her tears; she too
expected a rabbit out of the hat.

'I'll do whatever I can ... if I could ...' said Barbara
hesitantly. 'I ... we expect to be leaving the village soon.'

Mrs Dean covered her face and her shoulders shook.

There was little Barbara could do. If she could, she
would have washed her hands of the whole thing. But,
of course, she couldn't desert the girl like that. She

agreed to keep April busy in the week as long as she could; and Mrs Dean would after all have to give up her weekend job in Redcliffe. She had two weeks' notice to work out. Barbara would be about that long. After that . . .

Barbara's manoeuvres were nearing their completion. By this time she felt in regard to her husband as a person might feel standing at low tide with a sharp stone in one hand, and a limpet exposed on a smooth rock. One swift blow . . . Her husband had come to understand the situation. His wife would be kept in the manner she had married into. His mistress, if he wanted her, was his own private business which should not and would not interfere with the running of the household. And if he didn't like it . . . down would come the rock. The directors of the bank had made that very clear. She was expecting a letter any day now.

The letter arrived two days later; total capitulation. Everything would be as it was. His only condition now – his only request, almost – was that they live together. He had only enough to pay for one well-to-do household – one big house, one set of maids, one cook and so on. He had no wish to live without these necessary luxuries in life. Barbara understood. A man in his position had to respect appearances; he could hardly live in a cheap household, with or without his mistress. She had no intention of asking the impossible, although there would, of course, be no question of their living together as man and wife.

For this she had plotted and planned. The winning of it pleased her, but the life it offered her was not so pleasant. Like Tony, Barbara had enjoyed this new life very much more than she had expected to. She enjoyed living on her wits, she liked the intrigue of putting pressure on her husband. She liked living with her son in a small house, coping by herself, making a splash in the village as a single woman, beautiful, unconventional and clever. And she enjoyed spending the day with David Price.

David had said nothing to her, but the feeling between them was warm. She thought he really might ask her again to marry him . . . If he did and she accepted, it meant few servants, maybe just a cook and a maid. She would perhaps have to help the business; she'd like that; she felt she would make a good business woman.

On the other hand, did she love him? Barbara had no idea. Perhaps love was something that formed slowly; but she used to think that once about her husband. David was different; she had loved him, once. Maybe he had no such thoughts. But if he did ask, what would she say? That option alarmed her. But she would certainly consider it, given the chance.

12

April was scared – of the boys, of the village, of being deserted. There were demons all around her. She was also scared she might be pregnant. This thought was present in her mind all day; it made her spirits sink into the ground the second she woke up and she could never forget it for long. Her next period was two weeks away; she had that long to wait. If she was, she understood very well it would be the final straw. They would find a home for her and there would be no more days on the river. Partly because she felt so filthy, partly because she was so anxious, partly because she had this secret from him, Tony had turned overnight into a stranger to her. After what had happened she could no longer be close to anyone, but what else could Tony be but close? Barbara did her best not to leave them on their own but when she did it was horrible. Once or twice he tried to kiss her. She waited as quietly as she could until he had finished. It seemed to him that the gap between them was of her making. In fact she could do nothing about it . . . not yet. But she had no intention of letting it last.

Of course, all the village quickly came to hear her version of events. Some – the vicar, April's friends – believed her. Others such as Riley scoffed at the idea. But everyone agreed it made no difference. If it was untrue, April was spreading rumours about the poor boys that could get them into serious trouble; if it was true, then it was her leading them on that had got both her and them into this mess. No one wanted the village to be associated with this sort of thing. April would have to be dealt with, and soon.

One afternoon towards the end of the week, Barbara was out shopping with April and Tony when they ran into Tad on the road. He swaggered along with a friend. He grinned and nodded familiarly as he passed.

Barbara turned to ice. 'We haven't decided whether to go to the police or not yet,' she said coolly. 'Five years' hard labour at least, I'd have thought . . .' Tad's face fell and he almost crawled away. He was confident he had escaped that. He had convinced himself with his own mouth.

'It's our word against hers,' he told Joe grimly later that night. They agreed, but Barbara had scared them. They were that much more unlikely to pester April again, but it gave April herself no joy to see Tad's face dissolve under the threat. They had made it very clear the whole time it had been going on what they would do if she told. She saw him glance vindictively at her before he went on his way. She was certain he would find a way to take his revenge, and she was certain she knew how he would do it.

Over the past weeks April had grown bored with her various pets. The rabbits had turned into pie, the magpie and goldfinches had flown away, the snake slid back into the rushes where he was caught. Only Silas and Sissy remained, still living on the lawn outside the station house, roped by their feet to the dog kennel and feeding on scraps of bread and weed pulled out of a pond in a field half a mile away. April had been hoping to keep them till the following spring, when they might have mated and laid eggs, but now she convinced herself that the boys would take their revenge on the swans that Friday or Saturday night while her mother worked in

144

Redcliffe and she slept on cushions on the floor in Barbara Piggot's bedroom.

Silas would be kept inside, but it was impossible to move Sissy; she was as wild as the day they caught her and went mad if anyone came near. If she was dragged by her tether inside, she would beat her wings and fly into the walls. Worse, old Silas was terribly possessive of her and if anyone went near her he flew at them. Reluctantly, April decided that Sissy at least had to go back to the river.

They did the deed on Friday afternoon, before the hooter went at the boatyard. She waited until they had finished washing the dishes after lunch, then she took Tony's hand. He looked curiously at her and she tugged him and nodded to the door.

Tony thought she wanted to be alone with him. 'Just half an hour,' he begged his mother.

Barbara sighed. 'It'd better be half an hour . . . and no hanky-panky,' she scolded.

Tony would have argued, not at the conditions but that she felt she needed to tell him. But April tugged urgently at his hand, and the two of them walked down the short stretch of road to April's house.

Sissy opened her beak wide and hissed and hid herself right at the back of the kennel when they came near. Old Silas opened his wings, lowered his head and took up guard before it. Tony realised what she wanted.

'But why?' he demanded.

April wouldn't answer . . . it was too hard to get across and she had no wish to, anyway. Explanations were meaningless; she had other plans for Tony.

They had to cut the old swan's tether and tie him up under the apple tree in the garden before they could begin. April crept up behind the kennel and managed to cut the tether a few feet away from Sissy's foot. They beat the back of the kennel with a stick for a minute before she suddenly dashed out in a panic and stood blinking angrily in the sunlight, wings up, ready to fight for her life.

For almost a minute they stood watching her. Tony began to shout and make short runs at her and suddenly she ran across the lawn, flapping her wings. She collided with a rose bush and got all tangled up. Then in a furious clatter of wings she pulled free, found the gate and went hurtling up the road, feet paddling the ground, wings beating, until at last she found the air and flew straight down the road. It was odd seeing her in the air after she had been bound to the ground for so long; she looked like a strange child flying. She almost reached the village before she knew she was free. Then she changed direction suddenly, turned a sharp circle and flew strongly away, back down to the river with the yard of tether hanging behind her.

It was not wise to leave that lead on her, but Sissy was lucky. Three days later on the other side of Redcliffe, a fisherman found her with the lead tangled in a hawthorn bush. He cut her loose with great difficulty and got a bloody arm for his efforts. If he hadn't the foxes would have discovered her that night.

Meanwhile, April still had Silas to deal with. He was upset when Sissy flew off and tried to follow her. April decided on the spot that he should go loose, too. She untied his foot but he didn't know what to do and kept waddling between the familiar and beloved kennel and the gate, where Sissy had disappeared. In the end they wrapped him in a blanket and carried him down to the jetty. There, they bodily threw him off into the river. He fell out of the blanket sideways into the water, but quickly righted himself and sat there looking surprised. He hadn't been afloat for years, but he liked it at once. He shook himself, wagged his tail, eyeing the jetty and the nearby mud banks anxiously. Then he began to float majestically down river.

Tony wondered if April might cry at losing her favourite but she showed no emotion. The swan slewed in the current and ran into a bank of mud. Then he pushed off and paddled energetically away. April briefly took Tony's hand and led him back to the house.

They all spent a cosy evening in the parlour. Barbara asked April to build a fire out of paper and twigs and when it was going, flung in the fir cones to make bright, aromatic flames. They had to open the window because it got too hot. They played cards, drank tea and Barbara sang. April could hear almost nothing of the songs, but she laid her fingers curiously on the older woman's throat to feel the vibrations. She glanced at Tony and smiled, enchanted, before turning back, absorbed in feeling the music.

When they were left alone briefly, Tony did not go near her. April stayed where she was by the fireside, watching the cones crumble into glowing ash. Each watched the other secretly.

Later, Barbara set Tony some German to translate and gave April letters to copy. April could read if she had to but her writing was awful. She sat next to Tony and made the difficult little shapes with her fingers. She wondered, maybe she should write a little message to him . . .? But she was ashamed of her writing and wasn't sure she could do it with nothing to copy. She covered her work with her arm and frowned in concentration. But Tony peeped and saw; she was writing his name.

In bed, on a line of cushions under the window by the side of Barbara's bed, April watched the pale line of light from the gas lamp on the pavement outside shining through the curtains. Much later another, paler light joined the gas light, where the half moon dipped past the window on its way across the sky. April waited.

She was worried she would fall asleep lying there warm and sleepy, but she did not make a noise or get up and walk around. She waited long after Barbara had come to bed, and only when she had been still for a long, long time did April slip the covers off her legs and creep across the rug towards the door. Then she tiptoed across the landing to where Tony slept.

In the middle of the night, in the dark, out of reach of anyone, with nothing between them, April felt sure that the wonderful flower which had blossomed and closed would open again. In bed where you were only yourself the love would come back. April wanted there to be nothing between them ... no words, no secrets, not even skin. Here they could touch and there would be no need for words because their bodies and hearts would say everything. In that closeness, Tad and Joe would be driven out of her.

April wasn't thinking particularly of sex. But if that's what love demanded – and she supposed it would – then that is what they'd do. It was called making love.

Tony woke up as she came across the floor and sat up suddenly. He reached out and touched her hip, her warm skin under the thin cotton nightdress. With a quick movement, April pulled the nightdress over her head and stood naked. Tony moved over to make room and she climbed in next to him. They embraced. When she touched his face and felt that it was wet with tears for her she could have laughed for happiness because she

148

knew it was going to work ... everything was going to work. She had understood her heart, his heart. She was wise to all this. Then the door suddenly opened and Barbara stood staring at them by the quivering light of her candle.

See how far it had gone! She had thought she was in control of things, but see how far it had gone ...! Tony had betrayed her, told her this was not going on; April had betrayed her – and in her own house! She took the girl back and put her to bed but could not sleep herself. She locked the door from the outside and went downstairs.

On the landing Tony called her.

'Go to sleep,' she hissed.

'We just wanted to be on our own ...'

'On your own! Go to sleep!' she hissed, livid with rage. Is that what they called it ... being on their own?

Downstairs she made herself tea and paced agitatedly up and down, waiting for it to brew. What on earth should she do? Suppose the girl was pregnant ... God! They had sworn to her again that they'd never done it, but was she supposed to believe that? After this? They'd spent weeks alone together on the river; as soon as they had the chance the girl was off to his bed. Oh no, she wasn't born yesterday. They had to be separated before more damage was done, that much was clear. The worst of it was it was all her fault. Telling him about his father and about Uncle Bob – he was too young, far too young. She'd thought he'd understand but all he'd done was imitate them. She'd thought her son had more sense. The girl must have led him on, taken advantage. He was only fourteen for Heaven's sake ... it wasn't even legal!

She was so angry she knocked over a vase of honeysuckle flowers standing on a small side table in the cramped parlour.

'Damn . . .' She wiped the water off the table with her hand and stuffed the flowers back in. What on earth was she going to do?

The answer lay in the drawer in the front of the little table. She wiped up the water with a handkerchief and took the letter from her husband out, shaking off a couple of drops that had found their way inside.

The vicar had been right – the boy needed a father. She had, of course, discussed her options with him in confidence. He had talked of family, of duty, of reconciliation. Not of love. Was it too late for that? But how could Tony look up to his father now, after what she had told him? How stupid she'd been! But she had been angry, hurt. She wanted him to share her hurt. She had been selfish, of course.

Whatever, it had gone far enough, this holiday by the river. It had seemed like that, a holiday, to her, too. A week ago she thought she was being clever and helpful – to April amongst others. But was it surprising that the local lads wanted their bite of the cherry when Tony was having his? He had done the girl no favours and neither had she; it was time to get out.

Barbara did not relish the idea of going back to her husband. A freer, lighter life beckoned. If she had her way in a perfect world, she would wait, spin the summer out and see what developed between her and David. But it wasn't fair to do that . . . not fair to her husband, or to Tony, or to April.

That Sunday, David was coming to tea. She would tell him what she had decided – that her husband had asked her back and she had no alternative but to accept. No alternative. That was as near as she could get to saying that she might not do it if another alternative was provided. And if he did offer . . . Barbara was not sure. It would be a brighter life and perhaps a better one. The only problem was that the life with Elliot depended on home, wealth and convention, solid dependable things, despite this recent upheaval. Her life with David would depend on something so much more unreliable – his heart, and her heart. Such frail things to build a life on! But she would tell him and if he did ask, she would see what her heart told her.

First thing after breakfast next morning, Barbara left Tony in the house and took April down to the Post Office. It was obviously impossible to leave them on their own for a minute. There she sent a telegram to Mrs Dean in Redcliffe: 'COME BACK AT ONCE.' She sent Tony out on his own for the morning and kept an eye on April in the house herself. She was taking no chances. She gave the girl chores, one after the other, didn't talk to her or tell her what was going on. April performed the work dumbly, like a stricken beast.

Mrs Dean arrived at ten, having dropped everything and caught the first train she could. She had feared some awful disaster and was almost relieved to find out what it was. She agreed with Barbara – what choice had she? – there could be no question of the girl staying on with them now. Mrs Dean would have to take care of her girl, job or no job. She nodded grimly and herded April back home. Indoors, she sat down and wept. She loved April and she saw no hope for her, none at all. April sat by her side. For once the two of them wept together.

Until David came to tea on Sunday afternoon Barbara

had to bide her time. She felt as anxious as a schoolgirl – she had no idea what she wanted; there just hadn't been time. She had already left her husband's letter unanswered for too long. She had thought it a good idea to let him sweat for a while but now she started to fret that he might change his mind, so she sent another telegram on Saturday afternoon: 'APOLOGIES FOR DELAY. WILL ANSWER FIRST THING MONDAY.' She walked to the Post Office with Tony; she didn't trust Mrs Dean to keep the girl away from him. Tony watched her send the telegram and wondered; but she told him nothing – she had told him too much already – and he didn't ask.

When David came to eat the cake she had baked and the sandwiches she had cut for him, they talked politics, weather, about the plants Barbara had put in the little garden over these past weeks. After the cake she sent Tony out, poured more tea with a shaking hand and told David what had happened, what she had decided. He listened quietly, and fiddled with his cup.

'What a pity about April,' he said. He began to talk about how bright she was and how she could make anything of herself if given the chance. 'The way she's come on these few weeks... amazing. And she's had no school or anything.' Barbara nodded agreement and waited. David sighed. What a stupid thing to happen. God knows what sort of monster she'd turn into if she got into care, but what else was there? He pulled a face, sipped his tea. Then he began talking about his shops. Business was down. He'd been thinking about opening another branch in Colchester, but he'd have to wait until things perked up now. Really, things were getting bad, terribly bad. He was going to have to lay off staff. No one had any idea how it was going to end...

David talked on nervously. He said nothing about himself and Barbara. There was no offer. Barbara nodded and sipped her tea to hide her disappointment. Yes, she was disappointed. She was going back to her husband and she was disappointed.

April had no idea how but she had to find a way to show Barbara what she was, who she was. She wasn't the slut she seemed. She felt that she deserved someone to give her a hand out of the mess she was in and she had hoped – believed – that Mrs Piggot would be the one to do it. Hadn't she grown up? Hadn't she helped them? Hadn't she shown how she could be just like them, as good as them? She couldn't believe that Barbara was going to drop her now. The trouble was, even if she had words she didn't know how she could explain what she had been trying to do in Tony's bed that night.

There had been so little time before Barbara came and caught them but there had been no doubting that everything was still there between them. She would wait a day or so; but orders or no orders, she would see him again. She was certain of that. Meanwhile, and that apart, April wanted to be good. She was in trouble now, but she wasn't wild any more; they'd see. She was a real person, she could do as she was told, mostly. All weekend and all that week she promised herself she would leave the river alone because the important thing now, the really important thing that was getting more important all the time, was to show that she was as real as anyone else, so that someone would offer her the chance she needed.

Her mother took a week off work. She pretended to be furious that she had to waste her holiday just keeping an eye on April, but what really scared her was that she would soon have to go back to work; she had no option. What of April then? Her girl was no longer safe in the pretty little village by the river. Everything was closing up around her.

On Monday she called on the Piggots while she was shopping to see what was happening. When she came back April was at the sink washing clothes. She glanced up and then back at the water, lost in thought. Her mother banged the door, watched the girl's face as she bent over the sudsy water, shrouded in steam.

'They're going,' announced Mrs Dean. She watched April's face. April frowned and glanced anxiously at her. 'They're going!' repeated Mrs Dean. April stared back at her. She looked terrified.

'What did you expect? Did you think they were going to take you away with them?' scoffed Mrs Dean. She came over and began lifting the clothes up to run them through the mangle. Her girl looked destroyed. 'They've got their own lives to live, do you think they can hang around here teaching you table manners forever?' demanded Mrs Dean. She began to wring the washing out, pushing down hard on the mangle. She was angry because she, too, had allowed herself to hope. But April had gone too far, done too much, hoped too much. 'You scared them off,' she said brutally.

April said nothing. A tear fell off her nose and her mother was touched because April had been strong for so long, and now she was helpless and hopeless. She suddenly held her close as April began to sob.

'There, everybody's heart gets broken,' she told her. She hugged her daughter hard. April wept and wept. It wasn't just that. She was in love but like her mother she saw no hope for herself.

April spent the day in a trance. She was stunned. They couldn't be leaving her? Deserting her, could they? She couldn't believe that she had driven them away by wanting only to be close. They were her friends. They had helped her and she had helped them. But she needed so much more than they did.

April was certain that when Mrs Piggot and Tony left it would be all over with her. She couldn't go back to what she used to be; she wasn't a child any more. The boys would be waiting by the river and she would rather die, yes, she would rather throw herself in and drown than let them do that to her again. April was prepared to do that. She would never become captive; she would never be a victim. She had moved so far in these past weeks. She had run, she had flown, but not far enough. When Barbara and Tony left she would be alone again, a problem which the village was moving to solve. How could she escape? It seemed then to April that all she had in the world was pity.

She couldn't sleep. Towards dawn she formed a plan and suddenly got out of bed. As she had weeks before alone in the house, she made ready for a journey, but this time she was better stocked. Several thick blankets, a whole loaf, a big hunk of cheese, eggs – she gathered together all she could carry. She took her waterproof mackintosh, two pairs of shoes, a towel, and piled it all into the big rucksack under the stairs that her father had brought back from the war. Then she wrote her note and left.

Outside the weather was turning damp, but nothing like that was going to put her off. She moved heavily, weighed down by her stores, and made her way to the river where her little boat lay moored like an old friend to the jetty.

13

As soon as she found the note on the kitchen table, written in the scrawled, childish hand, Mrs Dean ran round to Barbara in a panic. Barbara had sent Tony away as soon as she knew it was news of April; she didn't let Mrs Dean say a word until she had watched him walk down the road. Mrs Dean, who had never seen her daughter write, was distraught enough to wonder if it wasn't a hoax and she had been abducted or something. But Barbara recognised the handwriting. And the girl had been pretending to her mother that she couldn't write! The words sloped dangerously down the page, childishly formed but clear enough: 'I am going to have a baby.'

There was certainly no question of telling Tony. Maybe he already knew, at least of the possibility. If it was true, he would *perhaps* be the father – Barbara stressed that perhaps. She would find out. If so, she would, of course, do what she could to see that the baby, if it came to that, was properly adopted by a good family.

Numb with shock, Mrs Dean nodded. Meanwhile, added Barbara, it would be best to wait a day or so before doing anything. No doubt April was sitting it out somewhere; she'd be back before long. Best to keep quiet about it until they were sure. It was scarcely to April's advantage for news of this to get about. Meanwhile anything she could do to help . . . Helen Dean nodded again and staggered back home. Things had moved so fast. April was lost.

On Wednesday afternoon Elliot was coming to pick

them up. Life would return to normal. True or not, her husband would never know. And Barbara decided too that Tony would not find out about this for a long, long time to come. Maybe never.

When his mother suddenly announced that his father was coming to take them back, Tony was horrified beyond belief.

'With him?' he demanded. His father? That beast? But amazingly it seemed normal, inevitable almost at once. He had got into serious trouble and his father was being called in. That's what it felt like. Meanwhile he had only one day to see April again. He would see her again. It was wholly unreasonable to expect him not to. If they had to separate, they at least deserved to say goodbye.

When Helen Dean called and he was sent away, he knew it must be something about April. He quizzed his mother later, but she said nothing, only that he was not to see her again. She tried to make a deal. So long as he did not see her again she wouldn't tell his father.

'I don't care what you tell him,' said Tony. He added instinctively, 'Does he know what you told me?'

Barbara looked warily at him. 'It would be best for all of us if he didn't know that. That's important,' she stressed.

Tony did not reply. But saying that had given him strength over her and when he walked out of the house a little later, she said nothing. He walked straight round to the station house.

He was about to tap on the back door but he heard weeping. He pushed the door open and to his surprise found it was Helen Dean.

'You're not supposed to be here,' she scolded, sitting up and trying to hide her tears.

'I came to say goodbye.'

'Goodbye?' Mrs Dean glared at him.

Tony shuffled awkwardly. 'Where's April? Can I see her?' he asked.

'Where's April? You tell me where April is . . .!' Helen Dean was suddenly angry and wanted her revenge . . . on Tony and on Barbara, who had deserted her with a pregnant girl while she and her precious son waltzed away back to never-never land. 'If you had the slightest thought for that girl . . . here, look at this . . .' She took the note from the table and thrust it into Tony's hand. 'She's run away, that's what. Where is she, he asks . . . She's run away, run away, just like you! Where is she, he asks!' Mrs Dean watched angrily, gloating. Tony read the note, the large, clumsy letters that had spelt his name two night ago. A baby.

'Your baby, your baby, that's what. Goodbye. And thank you, thank you very much . . .!' Mrs Dean began to scream and cry. Tony dropped the note and ran out of the door.

'Don't bloody bother!' screamed Mrs Dean after him. She choked on her words and began to wail behind him. Tony ran as fast as he could away from the village, away from the river, to the trees and fields inland. He knew at once where she would be. Hadn't she shown him where she went when she had to hide? No one else knew about it, he was sure of that. He was also sure that she wasn't pregant. She had told him she had not been raped; he had never slept with her. No. She was calling him and he had to find her before it was too late.

He knew from experience how lightly his mother slept

but that didn't matter – he'd run if he had to. While she was still downstairs he dressed fully and got back into bed. When his mother went to bed he heard her outside his door, listening. Then a noise . . . a key turning in the lock. She was expecting this.

He waited another half an hour, then he got up and checked the door. Locked, as expected. But the climbing rose was on a trellis right up to his window and the downpipe was only just out of reach. Tony swung himself out and dug his feet into the spiky rose. He found the thin wood of the trellis. It gave under his weight, but he was able to struggle across to the downpipe and then he was on his way down, pushing through the runners.

He was halfway down when he heard his door lock go; he hurried, slipped and fell a few feet through the thorns. She was at the window now.

'Tony! Come back!' She was begging him. He just let go and fell the five or six feet to the ground, scratched and bleeding. His mother ran out of the room to intercept him but he was off, running along the empty street and round the back into the bushes behind. He kept on running after he heard her at the front door, calling him furiously in a hushed voice for fear of alerting the neighbours. She came after him a few steps down the road, but she knew she had lost him already. By that time he was well away, over the hedge and running through the dark field. He tripped and lay still for a few minutes. When it was clear she was not following, Tony picked himself up and made his way quickly round to the jetty.

There were always a few rowing boats tied up by the jetty. April's, of course, was gone, but tonight there were two more. He had no idea who they belonged to but he'd be back by morning and no one would miss them . . .

no one would even know. The tide was out, the boats were resting on the mud. Tony had to jump down and drag the boat to the water's edge. He sank up to his knees, he was afraid he would sink beyond all trace or get stuck. But slowly he pushed and shoved, heaving himself out of the mud with the edge of the boat and pushing again, until at last it was afloat. Tony wallowed after it in the cold water and scrambled in, covered in mud and wet through. He was on his way.

Tony was not good with the oars. Rowing backwards into the seamless darkness he was scared of hitting something. After he found the deep water he made better progress and found himself skimming swiftly along, as quietly as he could . . . not for fear of being heard, but because it felt so still on the black water. Once, he got too close to the other side and scared the swans, roosting on the mud on the opposite bank. He was startled himself when they suddenly burst away from him in flight. The boat wallowed as he lurched back. But he recovered and pulled away from the shore again. After that he kept more careful watch. He learned to notice how the light from the sky was reflected less and with no ripples where there was mud. He didn't fancy having to climb back into the mud and push himself out again.

It was all so dark, so strange. Where was the landscape? Where were the islands? April's island was the third big one downstream but in the darkness he couldn't be sure whether he had missed one. But at last the third island slid by. He was half past it before he saw it. He dug an oar in the water and turned the boat towards it, as she had taught him to do weeks ago. The boat gently slid into the mud and Tony moved to the prow of the boat and peered into the dark clumps of trees. He could see nothing.

He climbed out and began once more to push the boat up the slippery, deep mud slope to the firm ground. He would have to search for her, but he couldn't leave the boat on the mud in case the tide came back and carried it away. Despite living by the river for weeks now, Tony never knew when the tide was coming or going, it always took him by surprise. He was sick of the mud and he'd gone in front of the boat where the land was firmer for pulling it when there was a noise behind him.

There she was. Tony turned to hold her, but she quickly laid hands on the boat. They pulled together until the prow rested on dry ground, nosing the tussocks of coarse grass that grew close to the water. Then April took his hand and led him into the trees where it was darker still. She had shown him her campsite before but he could never have found it in this light. Very quickly they were there; blankets hung over some branches, there were embers of a fire. April struck a match, lit a paraffin lamp and he saw her face.

They hugged. He was so wet April laughed and pulled a face. She gave him a towel, but all he could do was wipe some of the mud off his face.

Now they were together again what was there? They held each other, but Tony had nothing to offer. He held his face to the light and said carefully, 'Come with me.' She stared and he didn't know if she understood. He bent close up so that some echo of his words could reach her. 'Come with me!' he yelled. His words crashed violently in the quiet night. April shook her head sulkily.

'Do you understand? Come with me . . . come back home,' begged Tony. April shrugged; she understood but she wasn't coming back. Not yet.

They sat long minutes, side by side in the darkness,

April stared at him until it felt uncomfortable. At last she stood up. 'Go now,' she said. 'You go now.' Tony stood and held her to him tightly as if he would never let her go, although he would. She felt stiff and unfamiliar in his arms.

'I don't want to go,' he said. April squeezed him back but only to comfort him. Tony sought her mouth and kissed her but it didn't seem to work. She glanced at him briefly, gave a slight shake of her head and turned away.

The cold was back between them. April had no idea what she thought Tony would bring for her. She would have been miserable if he hadn't come. But now he had to go and she would be alone again.

Tony stepped off the mud into his boat. It swayed dangerously and he sat down suddenly. April leaned across as if to speak, and held his shoulder to breathe her warm breath in his ear... a silent promise. Tony kissed her face goodbye but she held onto him and hugged hard. Then she pulled back and pushed the boat away with her foot. For a second his face stared back at her, looking alarmed and pale in the dark. He turned to man the oars and the darkness closed around him. April began to trudge back to her camp but stopped short and sat a little in from the mud in the coarse grass to watch. The boat was already in darkness. All she could see were the ripples of the oars and boat's wake lessening as he passed into the darkness. She thought she would weep for him then but fear had turned her heart cold.

The clouds had thinned, the moon shone dully through. There was more light on the way back and he could see the vague shoreline, trees, bushes, the lights of the occasional house. The tide was with him. The glide from each light, long stroke seemed to last forever. After a while he put up the oars and the water pushed him along without a sound. He felt he was the only moving thing on the river – the ducks, the voles, the fishes, the other boats were all still and sleeping. Tony sat in the bow of the boat and waited while the water carried him back to Cibblesham.

The sky lightened as he came into the village. By the jetty the water had crept up and he had only a short way to drag the boat through the mud. He stood on the rickety wooden structure and looked down at it in the dirty morning light. The boat was filthy; whoever owned it would know someone had taken it after all. He turned and trudged back up the High Street to his house.

He hadn't realised how badly he had torn the rose about in his panic. It was half hanging off the wall. Inside, her face white with rage and anxiety, sitting before the ashes of a fire in the parlour, his mother waited.

'Well? Did you find her?' she asked bitterly. But Tony wouldn't tell her anything.

Tony slept half the morning. His mother was unable to. She lay in bed for a couple of hours and then got up to start packing. It was six o'clock. Elliot was due at two that afternoon.

She regretted this, all of it. She regretted that she had failed to keep Tony away from April, regretted that she had tried to. She regretted for herself and for Tony that her husband was coming that afternoon to re-start a life which had not been a happy one for either of them. And she regretted whatever fate awaited April. Now that all her manoeuvres had paid off, now that she had all she wanted – everything she wanted – she felt more helpless

163

than ever. But there was nothing else for her. She put the kettle on to make tea and began to dust the little parlour. She wondered if she would miss these little chores; probably not. She didn't have to do it now but she was determined to hand the house back in a decent state.

Elliot turned up at two o'clock, prompt as always. His wife and son stood in the parlour with their bags packed around them, waiting, watching him. All of them – father, mother, son – had found this first meeting unimaginable, but in the event it was only the same as it had always been. Barbara made a cup of tea, that was the only difference. They sat and drank it in silence.

'Had a good time, Tony?' asked his father cheerfully. Tony stared at him as if he'd asked him if he had been to the moon. Barbara coughed.

'Answer your father, dear,' she said nervously.

'Yes, thank you,' said Tony automatically. Barbara smiled and sipped her tea. Elliot smiled back.

Sitting in the back of the car ready to go, Tony sat forward suddenly. 'I'm not going back without April.'

His father twisted round to look at him, then glanced at Barbara in the seat beside him.

'His girlfriend,' she said lightly. 'Some girl on the river . . .'

His father snorted in amusement. 'You'll do as you're told,' he said matter-of-factly. He started the car.

Tony looked at his mother, her shoulders stiff with tension. He leaned back in the leather seat. She half glanced round and visibly relaxed. Yes, he would do as he was told . . . now and forever, he would always have to do as he was told.

It was almost the end of term. Tony's life restarted two weeks before the summer holidays but they made him go back anyway.

'Do understand, darling, there's so much to sort out,' begged his mother. Tony nodded. He spent that first night at home back in the old house, the very same one, as if there had been no time they hadn't lived there. The servants were different, though. The next day he was driven to school in a taxi. Before he went, left alone with his mother for a few minutes, she said quietly, 'Well done, Tony. I knew I could rely on you.'

'But what about April?' he asked eagerly. But she shook her head and said nothing more. None of that existed now.

Then, school. Worse than ever, because he'd thought he'd passed it by forever. The familiar sinking feeling as he sat in his grey clothes and the car moved slowly in through the grounds. He was abandoned here. School was where you had to struggle to be yourself, where you had to hide. He had no idea how he would cope but, of course, he didn't have to; it coped with him. He was back in his place. He had to sit in the lessons, field curious questions from his classmates, resume duties for Willis. It was all there inside him, all the time. It would last now forever.

Often in the classroom, on the playing fields, in the dorm. at night, Tony thought of the other life, which had seemed like a holiday but which he had thought would become real. He had been happy then for the only time. But that long secret space inside that had been full of warmth and light was now full of pain and loss. How fearful he had been at losing his father, his school. And how much he hated having them back!

At home, once the holidays began, he spent a week with his parents before he went off to stay with a friend of his mother's who owned a large house in Berkshire. He was terrified of going home, despite the break from school, but appearances made it all so easy. His parents seemed to get on no better, no worse than before. His father came and went to work, the servants quietly cleaned and cleared. He noticed now how often his father was away, that was all. When he asked his mother where he was going, she said lightly, 'Business, darling. Your father has to do a lot of work out of office hours.'

'Really?' he demanded.

'Really,' she said firmly. 'Really,' she promised, smiling at him with all her charm. He didn't believe her. The old silence descended between them. He was not to find out for many years if his father continued his affair, or if his mother ever secretly saw David. They played at happy families and wore their lives, and the lies of their lives, like garments which could never be taken off.

Tony had stayed with the Berkshire family before; there was a boy his age and a girl a little younger. His father drove him to the train and at the other end he was met by the boy, Simon, and his mother. The mother, Tony realised, must certainly know the whole story. He seemed to remember that she was one of those who had sent a precious ten pounds . . . so long ago, in a dream. She smiled and watched him as they drove back in a carriage pulled by a little chestnut mare. There were stables here, Tony remembered. He would go riding. The boy chatted – about school, about the holidays, about the things they would do together. He and Simon had always got on well.

'I'm glad you're here, the holidays get so boring,' Simon said.

166

'We're delighted to have you,' his mother agreed. 'It's nice to see you looking so well,' she added, as if Tony had been sick or something. Simon glanced enquiringly at her and she smiled blandly. Tony smiled back. He was glad to be here. Later he would tell Simon about it. His mother had told him not to tell a soul, but of course he would. He would boast how his father had a mistress and how his mother had outwitted him. But about April he would say nothing.

It was the middle of term. Everything had been this way forever, now. Tony did his work, slept in the dormitory, ran for his school house, fagged for Willis, who beat him if his bed wasn't properly made, if the toast got burned, or if he said the wrong thing. One day Tony would do the same things to another boy. Then there was a letter from his mother.

He recognised the handwriting at once, but he knew it was something different because the envelope was different, a big, buff coloured envelope. Inside was another letter in a white envelope, and a note from his mother.

'Darling Tony,
This was passed on to me for you. I see no reason why you shouldn't read it. You can reply, too, if you want to, considering the way things have turned out. But please, letters must go through the school . . . I don't want anything like it in this house. You can imagine what your father would say. It will have to remain our secret.'

Tony tore open the white envelope and read the letter inside. It was typed. Only the very last words were hand-written.

'Dear Tony,
I hope you do not mind me writing you. My teacher
Miss Stevenson is typing it out. My writing is still
no good. I know more words now but still not many
but she says she will help me fill in.

I wasn't (you know what) at all. You knew that,
didn't you? I came back the next day. After that Mr
Price came to my house and he said I could work
for him! He is my friend and I will always be grateful because he has rescued me. I found out that Dr
Lewis was going to put me in care. Now I do all
sorts of things.

Mostly I clean and tidy for him at home, he is
ever so untidy and dirty. He looks after me and I
go to school. My school is a special school for deaf
children, we are all deaf. I am learning how to write
and add up and everything. Most of the children
can speak much better than me. Miss Stevenson
says I will too but not yet.

Sometimes I help in the shop. I bet you never
thought I could work in a shop. I help make bicycles
and mend them, I am good at it. I want to help
serve people but they do not understand me. I am
even making my own bicycle! I see my Mum every
weekend. Sometimes I see someone from the village
but I don't talk to them ever.

I was scared of school at first after what you said
about school but my school must be different to
yours. I have made friends! I think of you very often
and all the good times we had in the summer. Now
we are both lucky and not just you. I still think your
mother is very nice even though she tried not to let
us say goodbye. But she never stopped us did she?

It would be very nice if you wanted to write to

me. You can write about anything and I would like it. I promise to write back to you. All those things they said about me weren't true, you know that.

I haven't met anyone else like you. (You know what I mean.)

AﾟriL xxx

READ MORE IN PUFFIN

For children of all ages, Puffin represents quality and variety – the very best in publishing today around the world.

For complete information about books available from Puffin – and Penguin – and how to order them, contact us at the appropriate address below. Please note that for copyright reasons the selection of books varies from country to country.

On the worldwide web: www.puffin.co.uk

In the United Kingdom: Please write to *Dept. EP, Penguin Books Ltd, Bath Road, Harmondsworth, West Drayton, Middlesex UB7 ODA*

In the United States: Please write to *Consumer Sales, Penguin USA, P.O. Box 999, Dept. 17109, Bergenfield, New Jersey 07621-0120*. VISA and MasterCard holders call 1-800-253-6476 to order Penguin titles

In Canada: Please write to *Penguin Books Canada Ltd, 10 Alcorn Avenue, Suite 300, Toronto, Ontario M4V 3B2*

In Australia: Please write to *Penguin Books Australia Ltd, P.O. Box 257, Ringwood, Victoria 3134*

In New Zealand: Please write to *Penguin Books (NZ) Ltd, Private Bag 102902, North Shore Mail Centre, Auckland 10*

In India: Please write to *Penguin Books India Pvt Ltd, 706 Eros Apartments, 56 Nehru Place, New Delhi 110 019*

In the Netherlands: Please write to *Penguin Books Netherlands bv, Postbus 3507, NL-1001 AH Amsterdam*

In Germany: Please write to *Penguin Books Deutschland GmbH, Metzlerstrasse 26, 60594 Frankfurt am Main*

In Spain: Please write to *Penguin Books S. A., Bravo Murillo 19, 1° B, 28015 Madrid*

In Italy: Please write to *Penguin Italia s.r.l., Via Felice Casati 20, I–20124 Milano*

In France: Please write to *Penguin France S. A., 17 rue Lejeune, F–31000 Toulouse*

In Japan: Please write to *Penguin Books Japan, Ishikiribashi Building, 2–5–4, Suido, Bunkyo-ku, Tokyo 112*

In South Africa: Please write to *Longman Penguin Southern Africa (Pty) Ltd, Private Bag X08, Bertsham 2013*